WOUNDED HEALER:

SAFE PLACES & OTHER THERAPEUTIC METAPHORS & ANALOGIES

by

Billy D. Haddock

Revised 2nd Edition ISBN-10-0-9669608-1-5

ISBN-13 978-0-9669608-1-5

DEDICATION

This work is dedicated to Mother. May flowers bloom in your name. It is also dedicated to you. May you become one of those flowers. In addition, this is dedicated to Scarlett, Buddy, Toto, Cosmo and the many other loyal four-legged companions I've enjoyed in this life. I trust you have found a safe, happier place.

Also, this work is dedicated to the wolves, which, along with the rest of us, will never be safe until humankind faces their predatory and violent nature, both individually and collectively.

Finally, this work is dedicated to God and God's People for the greatest good of all who have suffered and struggled to make meaning of life. I challenge you to question deeply, think for yourself, and find positive lessons in your painful experiences.

Contents

Dedication   3

Contents   **5**

INTRODUCTION   7

Chapter 1 - Birthing: Working through emotional pain   14

Chapter 2 - Birds & Bees: Understanding sex, intimacy, & spirituality   36

Chapter 3 - Adopting: How to take care of yourself   66

Chapter 4 - Mirrors: Viewing life's experiences as a teacher   97

Chapter 5 - Keys: How to empower yourself   121

Chapter 6 - Safe Places: Seeking emotional security   149

Chapter 7 - Bridges: Finding safety & support through life's transitions   176

References for Wounded Healer: 200

    APPENDIX A   202

    APPENDIX B   205

INTRODUCTION

The following stories are centered on a Native American shaman or medicine man, called *Gentle Wolf*. He is the alter ego of a fictional psychotherapist, Will McKinney, who spins a story with just enough reality included that the story could be biographical ... except for a subtle twist of psychopathology. In his case, *Gentle Wolf* is more like Will's trusted friend, than an evil other who competes for control of his personality. Through his alter ego, Dr. McKinney tells a personal story about recovery, growth, and human development. His voice originally came to him in the following dream:

I am an old man who has been arrested and jailed for leaving the scene of an accident without stopping to render aid. I have difficulty seeing in the dark and had simply not known I was involved in an accident. When I arrive at the jail, it seems that everyone there knows me, like I have been a regular visitor there. Memories of friendships with the old sheriff come to mind. My mind shifts from present to past as I fade in and out of consciousness.

I feel weak and keep passing out. Another inmate, an old Native American, comes around now and then when I am conscious. He tries to tell a deputy that I have a problem, but can't get his message across.

Lying there in my weakened state, I begin to feel a strong voice welling up inside me about to speak to the Native American inmate. I am about to deliver a message to him from a Native American entity or spirit guide attempting to speak through me. As the voice starts coming out, I awaken from the dream.

The Native American voice in the dream represents a part of the dreamer's personality that is older, wiser, and spiritual. It also represents a small part in a great resurgence of the Native American spirit. Like the nature of spirit, it is not bound to a specific blood line, but follows the path of least resistance. Our part in this is to learn to surrender to the spirit. This directive finds expression in the stories that follow. May *Gentle Wolf's* stories help you see, hear, and find a path of healing, growth and health.

This book entitled has evolved intuitively over the span of a therapeutic career. The work represents both evolution and erosion. The insights evolved as the career did. Like erosion, the gems located herein are polished naturally with the abrasive experiences of life and work.

The stories touch on the stages of a life's journey. It is both personal and universal, which, also makes it soulful. By providing intellectual and emotional insights, it increases understanding and represents about a third of the formula for progress in growth and healing. Another part involves action. The ancient notion of action-reflection is well established in many growth circles today. It is championed most by Fa. Richard Rhor at the Center for Action and Contemplation in Albuquerque, New Mexico.

This non-dualistic view (action AND contemplation) can help people more fully understand their lives. It invites people to think and reflect about what is going on in life and not just always be action people. In these days of rapid change and communications, the planet needs more people who are willing to be reflective and action oriented. Commitment, the third part of the formula for growth and healing, is unpopular these days. However, very little progress is sustained without commitment. 'Trying' gives counseling a bad reputation. People can 'try' for a while and show real progress. However, because they didn't commit to lasting change, they will have regressed back to the old, unhealthy habits within a short time.

Balance is the key. There is a need for a more balanced approach to management of individual lives, communities, regions, countries, and the entire planet. This book points toward that balance.

Why do people resist reflection and contemplation? It may be because they do not like what they see in themselves, their families, and the world around them. For example, the adult generation avoids looking in the mirror to understand our children who are at such elevated risk. The United States is among a minority with a narrow view of what's wrong. This is because they do not slow down long enough to see the reflection of themselves in their children.

Why do they not slow down? The modern world is in 'speed up' mode. Perhaps this is because they were programmed by their parents to measure success and self-worth against performance. A performance-based sense of worth reduces humankind to ant-like behavior, chasing the clock, and constantly in a state of doing. With stressed and fatigued bodies, confused minds, and empty hearts, people flock toward churches, therapists' offices, new relationships, or more compulsive and addictive behaviors in search of the ultimate quick fix. The spirit invites us to slow down, sit for a while, relax, and let it fill our emptiness. As we learn the discipline of contemplation, we discover fulfillment in being and doing and understanding.

Gentle Wolf, functioning like a conductor of an orchestra, represents that older, wiser part of McKinney's personality. He uses a creative approach to tell his personal story and talk about health, healing and growth as he incorporates ecology and Native American beliefs. *Gentle Wolf* draws from his nighttime dreams and uses past experiences to develop metaphors or analogies that help organize his message around everyday symbols. He is a Native American shaman who both instructs Will and is Will. He extracts a broader wisdom from the personal events of his life. Will's overall personality, functioning like an entire orchestra, provides supporting information and guidance in identifying and overcoming obstacles to the healing process.

Some people think there is too much emphasis placed on past childhood hurts. Others think we blame our parents excessively. However, when we match the negative events of the past with positive lessons for today, a balance is created between doing, being, and understanding, that provides personal stories with universal lessons. We find a way of remembering that brings healing and honor without undue blame.

My favorite Franciscan priest, Fa. Richard Rhor, says this about religious language, which also applies to therapeutic language:

"... religious language is metaphor by necessity. It's always pointing toward this Mystery that you don't know until you have experienced it. Without the experience, the metaphors largely remain empty. I think this has led to the ineffectiveness of much organized religion. The metaphors religions use are usually true, but we too often defend the words instead of seeking the experience itself."

He goes on to say:

"The word metaphor comes from the Greek and means "to carry across"--to carry a meaning across, to carry you across. If you're still living mostly out of the left brain, you think that the word must perfectly define. But the right brain realizes that the better way to describe the moment is through a metaphor, indirectly."

Metaphors and analogies are useful comparisons that can enhance our understanding of life and lead to deeper meanings. Both are symbols that connect outer Therefore, metaphors and analogies are useful for anyone taking steps down the path of personal and spiritual growth. I hope you find these helpful in finding your way toward healing.

This book begins with a chapter that focuses on the importance of working through emotional pain and finding meaning in suffering. It uses *Birthing* as an analogy to emphasize the benefits of facing your pain and working with it until you grasp the meaning it carries. Chapter 2 focuses on the importance of seeing the link between sex, intimacy, and spirituality. It aims at helping you understand how to achieve more intimacy in your life by using *Birds & Bees* as a comparison. The next chapter emphasizes self-care using *Adopting* as a way of introducing total care of soul, heart, mind, and physical environment. Chapter 4 is about learning from present and past experiences, including positive and negative interactions with other animals. The concept of *Mirrors* is used to increase insight into using life experiences as a teacher. In the next chapter, *Keys*, is used metaphorically to help you find and claim the personal power necessary for making free choices in your life. Chapter 6 focuses on the importance of looking inward and upward for emotional security and explores our attachments to people and places by using *Safe Places* analogously. This chapter also tells how *Gentle Wolf* came to know his Indian name. The last chapter focuses on the importance of finding and using safe passages through the transitions and cycles of life. I hope you find the *Bridges* analogy helpful in understanding how to use rituals and supportive people during times of change and stress. All of us are wounded in some manner. Through those wounds, we are empowered to serve. Henri Nouwen, another voice who speaks to me says:

"When our wounds cease to be a source of shame and become a source of healing, we have become wounded healers."

We move from victims to being empowered to serve and equipped to heal. Let us be wounded healers!

The material in this book may be read in order from beginning to end or, selectively, by spot-reading a specific chapter, depending on how the topics speak to you at the moment. A useful procedure, when reading therapeutically, includes reading through the entire selection quickly, then going back through the material slowly, making notes and reflecting on each section. Space for notes is provided at the end of each chapter.

A third look at the material might be to focus on selections one wants to review or fix in one's mind for later practice. Ideally, this book is best used as a supplement to an action-oriented personal growth program. It is not a substitute for therapy, although it may bring moments of insight that can contribute to the healing process. It can be used as a therapist-guided reading, which would most likely produce optimal results. Altogether, it can be useful for anyone struggling with issues of insecurity, emotional pain, intimacy, and self-neglect.

Ultimately, I hope that a career of work and insights in print can add value to more people's lives than any therapist could ever reach in person. Finally, may the self-knowledge and strength build hope in your struggle to survive and thrive.

Billy D. Haddock, Ph.D., 2017

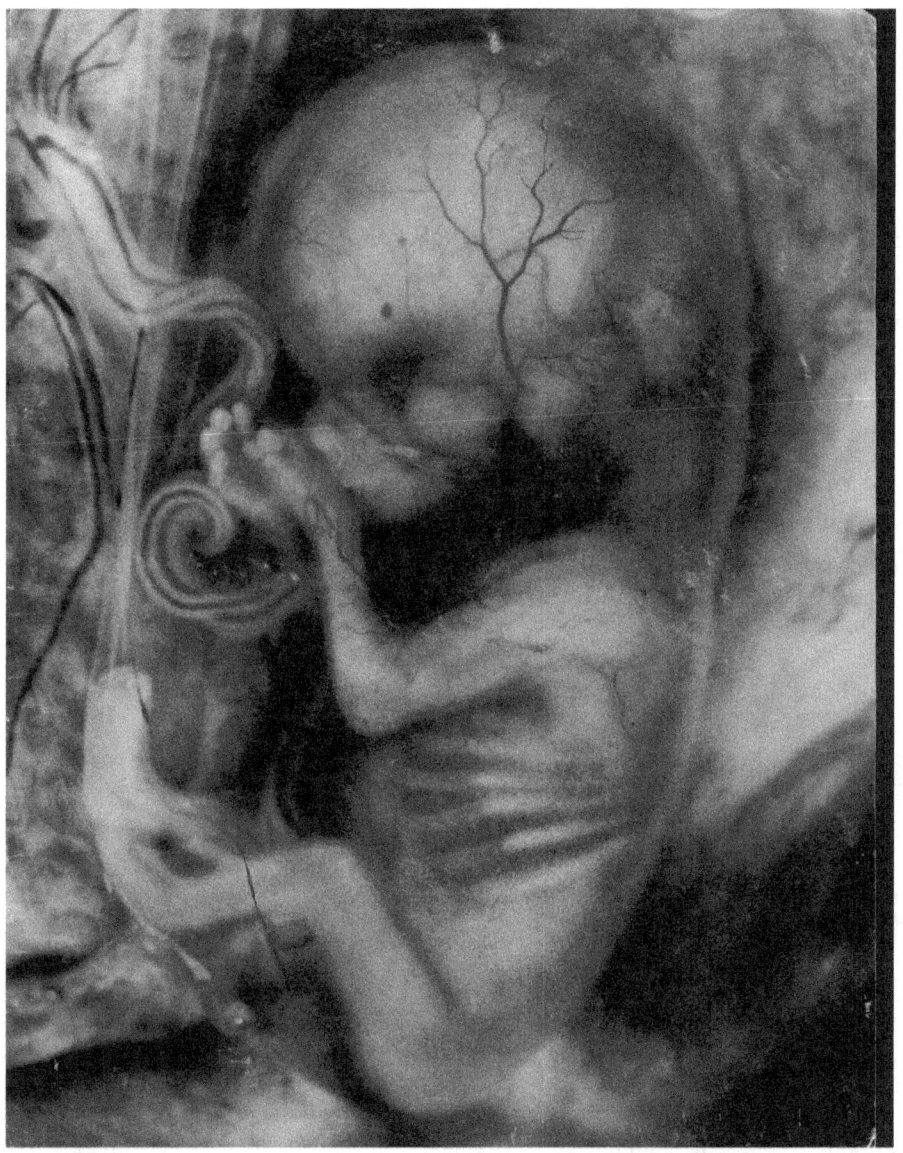

CHAPTER 1

BIRTHING: WORKING THROUGH EMOTIONAL PAIN

"She was a bleeder!" Those words echoed in my mind throughout my childhood. My mother bled to death from a collapsed uterus after giving birth to my youngest brother. It was an unexpected and untimely death. Because of this, I didn't get a chance to say "good-bye." Each one of us grieved silently.

I grew up thinking I might have inherited my mother's tendency to bleed, like a hemophiliac. I developed a slight phobia at the sight of mine or a loved one's blood. While doing family research many years later, I learned the true meaning of the expression. My aunt, who had often served as a midwife with mother, used the expression to mean that mother's uterus pulled away during childbirth and resulted in bleeding complications each time. This last time it completely collapsed, and she bled to death.

This experience was a personal lesson in the mistaken assumptions of a childhood mind. When people don't talk or grieve with others about closely held beliefs, they seldom examine their beliefs in the light of reason. Only after I started talking about that loss, did I learn about the connection between birth, pain and life in the process of healing. My mother left behind a widowed husband and seven children. I was four years old. I came to consider the scope of this trauma by thinking that it left a blank spot in my mind and heart when I thought of the word, *mother*. Another way I estimated the impact of losing her was that, 35 years later while having dinner with some friends, the unexpected remembrance of the anniversary of her death brought so much pain it took my breath away and left me momentarily speechless. A year later, after committing to the grief process, I still hurt on the anniversary of her death, but had made progress by actively working through the pain and grief. The next year, I experienced less pain around the anniversary of her death by talking about her with family, learning more about what she was like, and developing a healthier perspective about her death. I also began honoring my brother's birthday. I even had my first dream about mother! This work brought me to a feeling that the grieving was finally complete four or five years later, although it would be many years later before I was healed. I worked through the pain and learned from this slow, painful and very personal process. By this time, I was in my mid-forties.

Life went on after mother died. I grew up, lost my father to cancer my senior year in high school, went to live with a brother, on to graduate, lost all my personal belongings when his house burned down, finished two degrees in college, married, had a child, and entered the workforce as a helper. I worked as a counselor in correctional rehabilitation, completed a doctorate, got a divorce, and eventually established myself in private practice. After seven long years of living as a divorced man, I remarried. Long as they were, those seven years involved a lot of personal growth and healing. The world needs no more stories of pain and suffering. They are a dime a dozen. Without positive lessons learned, mine is just another sad story. Stories that generate hope are always in demand. However, you must demand the hope, squeeze the meaning, and search for the positive lessons from your life story.

Life is a cycle of birth, nurturing, maturing, creating new life, being of service and dying. It is the natural course of things. In my experiences as a therapist, I struggled with helping clients going through different changes in the life cycle. A major part of this effort has been to work through the pain, grieve the losses, and find positives in otherwise negative situations. Through this work, I found that these changes in the life cycle, often accompanied by pain and loss, permeate humankind's physical, mental, emotional, and spiritual existence. Pregnancy and birth are good examples of the powerful natural processes of change that have immense potential for positive as well as negative outcomes in life. Consider the analogy of birthing to discuss how people respond to pain as they grow, develop, and move through the cycle of life. The decision to birth a child is an excellent example of engaging in a painful process by focusing on a meaningful outcome. Just as physical pain in the birthing process can be a prelude to life, I view emotional pain and suffering as a prelude to new levels of maturity, peace and happiness. Therefore, I chose birthing as an analogy for learning how to work through the pain and suffering of life. If you are childless, you may have difficulty relating. Please be patient and stay tuned   It will be worth the effort.

Labor

The process of giving birth typically begins with the pleasure of sexual intercourse, even if it may be involuntary, one-sided or inconsiderate. However, it usually involves love. A sperm fertilizes the egg and a single cell is formed that locks in the energy and essence of life. Soon thereafter, a heartbeat begins. From there, many options are available. For example, the birth can be terminated early through abortion or miscarriage. If the decision is made to carry the baby full term, the birth can come prematurely, on time, or be overdue. It can be delivered through natural childbirth, or completed with surgical assistance.

During the pregnancy, the mother goes through major biological changes to accommodate the fetus. Along with this often comes an increased feeling of discomfort as the fetus grows and becomes more active. This discomfort heightens as the delivery begins with a series of progressively more frequent contractions, usually lasting from eight to 13 hours. As the contractions and expansions proceed into the second stage of labor, the baby moves down the birth canal and the pains become excruciating to the point of birth. At this stage, the mother can participate by bearing down or pushing following each contraction. Then a miracle occurs! A new life is born. The third stage comes after delivery. This stage involves the expulsion of the protective placenta, referred to as afterbirth, by contractions continuing after delivery. At this point, recovery and healing begins.

The analogy between birthing and working through emotional pain can be seen in certain key words that relate to the birthing process. For example, abortion has parallel meanings for how people avoid pain, whether associated with an actual unwanted birth or unwanted emotional pain. Contraction or expansion relate to knowing how to respond to pain (emotionally or physically). It's helpful to know when to give in to it and when to stretch and push harder. Breathing relates to the importance of remembering basic life-sustaining behaviors while struggling with painful experiences. The placenta can be viewed as a protective wall that we attempt to duplicate or retreat behind when faced with pain. Actual birth and the miracle of new life parallels how many people feel who work through pain and move on with their lives. If you have difficulty relating to this analogy, just remember you have participated in at least one actual birth. Watch for these parallels and relate with your life experiences as various aspects of birthing pain are discussed.

My role as a therapist is like that of a midwife. I am there to facilitate the process of emotional birthing and witness the magic of the moment, like that of an actual birth.

A therapist can also be viewed as playing the role of Lamaze coach by teaching relaxation and breathing techniques to provide guidance and support through the pain of labor. Fear of the unknown causes tension. Tension contributes to more pain, which causes more fear and contraction. Breathing and relaxation help break the cycle. The coach, while not involved in actual labor, can be there on the side to offer support, encouragement, and information.

Experiencing pain

Many people's search for love leads to childbearing. Love has two rhythms: passion and compassion. Passion is where two people care greatly about each other. The blood boils and the mind is filled with thoughts of the loved one. As they narrow their social circles and focus on each other almost exclusively, they experience a contraction. If the loving relationship goes well, they go forth with compassion for others, which expands their social circles again. Therefore, from the feelings of love that they have for each other, they can expand, grow, and go forth to shower love on everyone they meet.

Failures in the search for love naturally bring emotional pain. When relationships fail, people often feel rejected, abandoned, isolated, lonely, empty and defective. Broken relationships also have two rhythms: pain and healing. Pain, in the form of distress, discomfort, depression or anger, causes contraction. During painful times, some people isolate themselves from the ones who could provide needed love and support. This is because they have difficulty sharing current pain with others. They retreat to protect themselves. The contractions or isolating behaviors are often greater and more frequent as the pain increases. Increased pain, like stress, results in increased contraction, which squeezes off the channel through which love can flow, either inwardly or outwardly. Left feeling alone and abandoned, they tend to feel nobody can be there for them. Pain turns your attention inward. It makes you self-centered. Healing can only occur with expansion and being willing to push at the right time. This involves acting, focusing outward. These people must make a conscious effort to walk through the passage of pain and receive the healing that waits. It often takes a lot of faith, love, and a strong sense of purpose to walk through the pain. That's why we need the support of loved ones to get through it.

Aborting pain

In therapy, I have observed people who had developed major patterns of aborting emotional pain. Emotional abortion is a way to avoid the birth of a pain. People often attempt to prevent or expel a painful experience from their memory. Avoiding painful issues is common. For example, a few years ago, I was awakened from the following dream:

I am leaving my friend's house following an argument with her regarding how we will spend our time that evening. At the driveway as I am about to enter my car, a voice calls out to me twice. It isn't understandable, but sounds human. I give a questioning look at the cat and other animals nearby. They say the voice comes from the garbage and point to it. As I approach it, I see an aborted fetus wrapped in plastic. The heart is still beating prominently. I want to avoid looking at it. Then I awaken.

This dream had a powerful effect on me. It contained much symbolism and definitely caused me to give the abortion issue more thought and attention. I knew from previous training to consider that everyone in the dream is about me. With some interpretation I finally came to grips with that part of me that is like a newborn baby, totally dependent on others. I even owned up to that part of me that is like an unborn baby, totally dependent upon God.

I considered how I took on another's people pain. Sometime later I learned that many healers take on their client's pain in order to help with the cure. They often work with altered states of consciousness, interpretation of dreams being only one technique. Shamans deliberately alter their consciousness or go into a trance as part of their healing methods. It is safer than dreaming. With dreams, you sometimes cannot stop unwanted experiences or nightmares. When you voluntarily go into a trance, you are able to will yourself out of it at any time. Like so many life situations, having a sense of control helps reduce anxiety and fear.

Dreams are only one way the subconscious mind invites you to face painful subjects. At the most awkward moment, something can trigger a memory and the painful feelings come back. This is called a flashback. Experience the pain, move on, and leave it behind. Otherwise, it will call out to you in an untimely manner. Emotional abortion leaves its own scars. However, when the pain feels abusive or life threatening, abortion may be necessary. In either case, when pain is suppressed or avoided, it leaves a violation of the inner psyche unattended, retards healing, and inhibits growth.

~ 19 ~

The dream also reminded me how some people attempt to avoid certain responsibilities in their lives and seek quick fixes. Some avoidance patterns people use are largely unconscious defensive behaviors, such as denial of a problem's depth and impact. Denial in others is more obvious, in the case of drug and alcohol abuse. Seeking quick fixes sets the stage for the cycle of addiction. It begins with pain avoidance. Next, relief-seeking brings one to the use of alcohol or other addictive agents. Negative consequences result from excessive use of the addictive agent, ultimately leading one to more pain. Then the cycle continues, spiraling downwardly. In these cases, this instinct to avoid pain often blocks the way to greater growth and development. In addition, some people get stuck in a cycle of pain and addiction while they bring someone else down with them.

Native Americans are known for their sensitivity to alcohol. As a group, they have had widespread problems with alcoholism. They are genetically sensitive to addictive agents. However, their way of life was taken away. Can you imagine how much pain native people suffered when their families were split apart and land and culture were taken away from them? In extreme cases of suffering, the Great Spirit provides people with a means to survive. People use survival mechanisms long past their usefulness and to a point of excess. This happens repeatedly all over.

I can only imagine how much pain a parent endures when a child dies. It often splits parents apart. Others retreat into alcohol or other addictive agents and never come out of it. Whenever an alcoholic comes into recovery, he or she often must face the pains that have been anesthetized.

In working with a lot of men in therapy, I noticed how some avoid pain by emotional numbness. From these observations, I came to believe that many men (and women, too), who are culturally programmed for competition and divisiveness, have become desensitized to the dull pain of separation and loneliness.

Desensitization begins after birth following a brief feeling of connectedness with the mother. Men are systematically taught to be alone and stand alone as a "man," for example. They stand as a little man at first and work from there. They are taught not to admit to weakness or loneliness, lest they be judged less than a man. So, they go forth in life, searching for love, an antidote to the pain of loneliness and separation.

On the other hand, I observed people who seem to move forward in personal growth only when the volume of their pain is increased. These people seem to want to work on change only when they must, usually if there is a crisis in the making. Otherwise, they do what they want. Things are viewed as going well when there is no apparent pain and suffering. In either case, they must recognize emotional pain as a necessary part of the growth process in order to work through current and past hurts.

In summary, some people attempt to abort pain. Others erroneously believe they should be able to handle it all by themselves. When we experience an emotion, we sometimes feel it will never end. We mistakenly believe it will last forever when we identify too much with the emotion. Therefore, we resist the feelings, either by avoidance or by trying to hold on to them. Paradoxically, to resist is to exist, and what we resist will often persist.

Just imagine how the first woman having a baby felt. No one else was there to tell her what to expect or to explain what was happening. She probably thought something terrible was happening, such as death or some evil spirit that was inside her causing pain. Like this woman, many people can usually benefit from someone helping to explain what is really happening regarding their painful experiences. Knowledge of the process and having a keen sense of purpose helps people face pain, know how to cope with it, and work through it.

Facing pain

Losing my mother so early in life was very traumatic, partially because I was so close to her. She was a stay-at-home mom. I was a preschooler. She was quoted as saying that I would probably become a radio personality because I was such a 'babbler.' The greater trauma was losing touch with my essence, my inner child. In some weird way, I have come to connect this babbling part of me to my inner child. Losing touch with your essence is a trauma most people experience. It is more common than you think. The extreme trauma is when your personality separates from itself, dissociates and sees itself as separate from the inner child and other aspects of self. Therefore, dissociation is the extreme defense mechanism.

One of the main discoveries of therapy is that it is not possible to change self-defeating patterns of behavior just by wanting to. You must face the problems, learn a better way, and start practicing like your life depended on it. You outsmart your old, bad habits by maintaining awareness of what lies behind or underneath a particular trait, feeling, or action. Often breaking one pattern helps considerably in breaking others. You develop re-learning skills.

Therapy helps sort out a current painful experience from an experience of old pain. A current painful experience is something, which causes real pain and usually has a beginning, middle, and an end. It starts, people feel it, it finishes, they let go of it and carry on. An experience of old pain is an old tape playing continually inside, and whenever something recent reminds you of it, the tape plays its old tune at full volume all over again. You keep it going because it's a habit, you know better but don't do better, it's a part of you. Most of the suffering people have in their lives is a mixture of the old and current pain. On the one hand there is the real existing pain and on the other, there is the pain from the past. They combine to create the felt experience and people are unable to tell them apart.

So, they get a double dose of pain that feels like a hard labor, or a miscarriage, one they cannot get through. It keeps recycling. These people have stopped short of the miracle right at this point.

This is the place where knowledge of birthing techniques is important. There is a proper way to push at the right time that helps to get through the pain. In addition, it is helpful to remember to breathe and pay attention to the pain.

Sometimes, during pain, fear, and expression of deep emotions, people hold their breath or forget to breathe. They often have to be reminded to keep their airway open and breathe slowly from the chest or even to pant-blow in an active manner to control the urge of an ill-timed push. Breathing techniques also remind us to provide for our basic life-sustaining needs while working through painful experiences. These techniques are valuable tools which can be applied to the unique needs people bring to therapy.

Therapy separates the old pain from the current pain and helps people work through each of them. This involves releasing it, understanding it, letting go of it, and transforming it in some way so that the energy locked up in it can be used for something better. Are you having trouble letting go of either pain? Just sit in it a while longer. When you get tired of it, you will let it go or get help. When this happens, you are then left with just the real current experience to deal with. This makes the process of birthing the present pain possible and much easier. If the pain is life-threatening, then medications or a C-section may be needed. In either case, a physician is needed to assist the mid-wife. With help, you can even get through the birth with a short labor and no scars. It also leaves you with new experiences and skills in working through future pain constructively.

In many ways, I thought my mother was a victim of circumstances: of place - living in a rural area near a small northeast Texas town with limited medical services; of <u>time</u> - the early 1950's offered few modern medical procedures and technology, including birth control options; and of <u>persons</u> - the doctor who delivered the baby, the father who conceived the baby, or the innocent baby himself. However, instead of blaming, I learned to honor the role of all circumstances and people in this event and look for the advantages and positive lessons. Only a spiritual viewpoint delivered me from the pain. I chose to see this tragic event as transformed by Divine Goodness to be used for growth and development. By shifting my viewpoint, I learned to affirm goodness in all circumstances. I made meaning out of my suffering. This only happened after I faced my pain.

Delivery

Psychotherapy is a major factor in shifting our emotional defense levels. It helps transform methods people use to protect and comfort themselves. During psychotherapy, rigid defenses are slowly abandoned and replaced by more flexible means of coping. We must honor rigid defenses because they shield our deepest and most painful feelings.

It is important to slowly transform the rigidity into flexibility, like a placenta around you. This is what emotional healing is about: learning safe and adaptive ways to work through pain and minimize unnecessary suffering to all concerned. In the meantime, we honor the defenses because they do protect and shield from the pain.

In making the transition from rigid to flexible defenses, people will experience some discomfort. However, it is important to avoid the trap of seeking quick fixes. While these approaches offer big promises, and can be helpful for some people, they often create unnecessary pain that feels abusive. To complete the transition to healthier defenses, people must consciously accept some degree of pain while setting limits. This is emotional regulation or self-control, a measure of maturity.

Accepting pain

Becoming a shaman, like any other process of becoming, involves accepting pain and dying to an old notion of whom and what you are. You give up your pain-based identity and become your future self.

Becoming your future self translates into the death of a way of life that no longer suits your new growth pattern. It can also simply mean letting go of old unhealthy habits. Many adults continue to react emotionally to pain as if they were still a little child. We must acknowledge our growth and adjust emotionally. An adult can handle pain much better than a child. This leads to taking on a new sense of self that is broader and richer, such as seeing your emotional and physical self as the same age. And, as time goes on, this new identity may also begin to seem small and restricting. People do expand further as they come to know the many parts that make up their sense of self. So, these people experience continued rebirth with a certainty that makes growth possible. The last step on this path is to leave the personal self for the greater self, sometimes called the higher self or transpersonal self. This opens the way for guidance from the best that is within us. It is at this point that people begin to realize that there is a Higher Power that is far more intimate with us than our parents could ever be. They come to know and honor that innocent part of self that depends on their Higher Power, like an unborn baby depends on its mother for its very existence. They come to identify with the precious child within.

The focus of the ego is survival. This is the reality of the ego. Most stress is generated by ego-threatening situations, not life-threatening ones. When people die, the focus of consciousness is no longer on the physical survival of the body. When the ego becomes convinced that the survival strategy is no longer working, then other options are considered. This happens most noticeably during extremely humbling situations, a crisis, or a near-death experience. During these times, the ego melts and the mind is willing to consider other realities or options. There is a letting go of old ways when the mind gets the message that something is wrong and thinks it is going to die. Consciousness seeks its own continuance; therefore, it considers other options. It is at this very point that people are willing to change, to learn skills necessary for thriving, not just surviving.

It is in letting go and in dying to old ways of being that people sustain life. This includes death in the service of the life force, like dying in the delivery of a child. A life ends so another can begin. Life is characterized by many losses. Each loss is a test that pushes against our emotional limits. In these series of tests in life, people are called to confront their fears and endure the pain with humility and courage. However, it is important to know your limits. Unless the pain of each loss is fully felt and worked through, it remains buried in the psyche like a festering sore that never heals. It exudes emotional poison. The poison must be transformed into a healing balm. As this happens, people experience acceptance and are born into higher dimensions of reality. If they resist, the journey of life can be a long, drawn out process with recycling periods of severe pain.

The process of changing habits has its version of pain and discomfort. It involves some confusion: dissonance between your head and gut-level feelings. Many people abort the pain at this point. To move forward, this pain must be accepted as part of the re-learning process. It's trial and error. To pass through this stage, people need supportive teachers. In addition, they must remember that learning takes time and each experience yields positive lessons.

If these lessons are learned well, people can emerge with a new sense of self that includes service to all of life. In other words, that which is birthed is meant to be given away at some point. Learning and sharing with others helps add meaning to the healing process. For those who desire to serve, growth and healing leads to becoming potential healers themselves. To take this step, people must learn how to embrace pain, experience it, and then release it.

Releasing pain

If you seek healing, be prepared to lose everything or abandon old, self-defeating beliefs. Healing is a ravaging force to which nothing is exempt. Therefore, to become who you are destined to be, you must be willing to give up everything you are.

All beliefs must be examined. For example, anything that you believe that is untrue or only half-true can harm you. Lies you believe can hurt you badly. As your original pain releases itself in healing, it destroys the realities, structures, and foundations you built in vulnerability, weakness and ignorance. Major shifts occur. You may face the fact that you deceived yourself and others. You lived a lie. At this point, although you may become painfully disillusioned, a door is opened to higher level realities. You see a higher truth. Ironically, only you can pay the price of having lived a lie. As you pay this price, you also get to experience the miracle of rebirth.

How can we release pain? Here are a few suggestions:

- Develop a lower threshold for pain. Stop ignoring it. Admit its presence. It's true that tough times can teach you perseverance, which leads to maturity. Feeling your pain also helps prevent a tolerance for unwanted treatment. Therefore, having a healthy sense of limits helps you know when enough is enough.
- Be still. Make conscious contact with God. Go slower to go faster. Get your head out of the sand. Seek guidance from others and be open to their advice. Balance being with doing and understanding.
- Realize that attention is selective. Fight your own inclination to see only what you want to see or to escape through distractions. Be mindful of what you are learning.
- Understand the cost of negative thinking and get rid of it. Do not give in to self-pity and bitterness. Get on prescription medications, if

necessary. Program your mind with thoughts that are true, noble, pure, lovely, and admirable. Make these your desires. Keep your focus on what you want and desire.

- Have your goal(s) and values clearly stated. Take the time to reflect on what you want. Develop a sense of purpose. Make sure it's in your best interests to want it. This will guide you as you release your pain.

Here are a few other things to remember:

- Come to believe: "I have a right to my own pain." "I also have a right to set limits."
- Deal with your feelings. If you don't then you will either go into a downward spiral or stay stuck in a holding pattern. Feelings can keep you stuck, as in fear, or move you toward your desires. Sort out the fear-based ones from the love-based ones.
- Feel the pain. It is not the pain that will destroy you: it is your resistance to it. Resistance to an emotion magnifies it. What you resist will persist. You can let it go a little at a time. Feel it now. Let the feelings live and they die birthing.
- Look for the hurt. Many people use anger to cover up the pain and hurt. Behind anger, there is hurt. Behind hurt, there is an unmet need or desire. Use your pain to teach you what you want. Make it meaningful.
- Seek support. It is helpful to have someone to listen to your pain and to hear what your losses were. Lean on somebody a little, but choose carefully. Ask someone: "Please hear me." People who tend to isolate and be alone with their pain are least likely to release it because they either won't seek help or rely on unreliable people.

Stress, discomfort, or pain usually precedes and accompanies change. Some people fearfully try to avoid pain and, sometimes, foolishly go to great extremes to avoid all pain, including never crying out in pain. Avoiding and resisting pain only magnifies it. At times, you must work with the pain and push even when it hurts.

In addition, you must learn to distinguish between constructive and destructive suffering. Abuse and neglect are other terms for destructive suffering. Constructive suffering is a passage to growth and healing. It has meaning and purpose. As people grow and heal, they become increasingly aware that they are living a life and have choices about how they want to live. Life rises to a new level of consciousness. Therefore, you can learn to surrender to constructive pain, work through it, grow from it, and develop more flexible methods of coping with it.

Remember, every birthing is different; as new days are born, new seasons are birthed, new pains are labored through, new realities are seen, and new relationships are created.

Recovering from pain

Some Native American people never mentioned their dead. They believed the spirits of the dead had no place in life. They advocated grieving in private. Many have continued these traditions, but too much silence can block recovery from grief.

After a release of the grief I carried for over 35 years, the long and tiring process of recovery began. How could I grieve as a little child? The little child in me didn't even understand the finality of death. My grieving was also blocked by the family's silence about my mother. They didn't grieve her death either. As I recovered, I faced what the real problem was, accepted what I needed to do to solve the problem, and worked on solutions. I started talking about the loss of mother. First, I talked with my sisters, and gradually, with my brothers and others. I admit that I hid behind the guise of doing family history research, but my intentions were honest.

Much of the recovery lies in a person's willingness to face problems, surrender the ego, and believe in the treatment. It includes investing some sweat equity, doing your homework. It also involves the belief that you are a part of a larger therapeutic system, which includes others, the natural environment, and some form of spiritual help. In addition, recovery calls for large doses of holding, caring, and simply having somebody to be there for you. I could have used more support in my journey. It's not like it wasn't there for me. I mistakenly blocked myself from it.

Who knows how much love a motherless child misses during a childhood? I hungered for a mom to attend family school functions with me. The child within you has a similar hunger for unconditional love and acceptance, for somebody to be there for you. For adults, recovery involves the lengthy process of learning to love yourself and others unconditionally.

Surrendering the ego is subconsciously associated with death. It is like disappearance. In a society that places much emphasis on appearances or image, to disappear is equal to dying. To enjoy life, we must be willing to die, to disappear. We resist because we think the pain of disappearance will last forever. If we fear disappearance will be permanent, then we resist it and we suffer more. This is why surrender is so important. Anyone who has ever surrendered the ego to humility knows how quickly selfishness and arrogance reappears.

Recovery calls for the development of new skills for coping with the inevitable pain stemming from the problems of life and using novel attempts to solve them. This is called re-learning. It involves 5 steps:

1. Education: Learning the new, better way and how to do it. This involves developing 'know how' and involves using willpower. If you just stop at this step, then you just become a 'know it all,' you know better but don't do better. Many people are knowledgeable at this level and love to tell others how to live.

2. Training: This involves lasting commitment. At the moment of implementing what you know about the new, better way, you must force yourself to just do it. At this point, you begin to build sweat equity, but first you must deal with the next step or you will give up.

3. Dissonance: This is a felt experience that often does not accompany the original learning process. It is a predictable step in re-learning. When you commit to changing habits, you are already an expert at doing it the dysfunctional way. So when you begin practicing the new behavior, it feels like a beginner again: uncomfortable, clumsy, awkward, stupid, weird, inept, etc. We call it getting out of your comfort zone. It's stressful, but good stress. It's like trying to sign your name in cursive with your non-dominant hand. It takes longer, and you are not as proficient. At this point, you must stay in your head. Habits are powerful, but not very smart because they've been relegated to the subconscious mind. Being mindful of the new, better way helps you overcome the dissonance. Habits are least action pathways. It takes less energy to follow the habits. It takes a tremendous amount of energy to overcome an old, bad habit. It's like trying to change the course of a river.

4. Experience: Over time, you begin to get the feel for the new, better way. It feels more normal. Gradually you begin to just do it and don't have to think about it as much. This is another way you measure the change: you do it in real time, and no longer must catch yourself and re-apply willpower.

5. Habit: When you are just doing it without deliberate effort, you now have a new level of expertise. You have a new, better habit. This process takes time, teachers, commitment, energy, and application of lessons learned. People cease to learn new things if they are not willing

to experience dissonance: feelings of clumsy, awkwardness, or ineptness. Therefore, cultivate the beginner's mind. It's okay to be a beginner again.

I have learned that if you center your life on those activities which will enable you to eventually do what you cannot do now with direct effort, then you can accomplish much over time. This is re-learning and leads to transformation. In some circles, it is called re-creating yourself. This is not new information. The scriptures said it long ago: Be transformed by the continual renewal of your mind.

Healing from pain

While I believed in healing, I guess it never occurred to me that I could have it. Healing was for my clients or more spiritual, faithful people. (Is this codependency or what?) Healing was for physical problems, not emotional. Maybe I secretly believed that this was not a wound that would ever heal. It was a blind spot, until someone who literally had committed her life and vocation to God suggested it was available. My eyes were opened to the possibility. I believed it was there for me, eventually. It happened, although it was gradual.

How do I know? I am moving on with my life without losing energy to that part of my past. My energy is spent serving God and his people. I am creative and productive. I am well, happy, and grateful. I have learned to honor my ancestors and stay in relation with loved ones in the unseen world. Earth is my mother. All of God's creations, the living creatures who inhabit earth, are my siblings. I belong here. This is my earthly home and family. The pain that made me self-centered has been transformed into a positive energy that serves for the good of others. This is how I know.

Healing is not perfection and does not occur in isolation. Healing functions like an orchestra. There are instruments whose music is just noise when played unskillfully or alone. When no one cooperates, or follows the lead of a conductor, that same noise occurs. Are the players absent when they are silent or noisy? No, they just know when to be quiet and when to play. They surrender to the lead of the conductor. This is what healing is like. When they warm up before the performance, have they lost their talent? No, they are just warming up and making sure they have control of the instrument. Healing is like the beautiful music of a talented orchestra. It's the blend of many instruments performing in a timely manner, both focused on and surrendered to the leadership of a conductor. Healing brings music to life. Healing reduces the noise of pain and suffering.

At a deeper level there is no life or death, only consciousness. This is the childlike essence deep in each person that, once contacted between two people, creates an intimacy that transcends death. As emptiness becomes form, a new life is birthed. When form changes or resolves back into emptiness, we are transformed. This is sometimes called death, other times called rebirth. In either case, there is movement toward meaning and purpose. As we move through life, there are many births, deaths, and rebirths, especially on the level of emotional maturity. The process of emotional rebirth creates in you the capacity to become intimate with all life, experiencing the joy, love, and laughter of a welcomed, healthy child.

Notes

CHAPTER 2

BIRDS & BEES: UNDERSTANDING SEX, INTIMACY, & SPIRITUALITY

Sex was not openly discussed during my teenage years. Intimacy was a private matter. Often, knowledge of things sexual was coded by a reference to "the birds and the bees." While people remarked about this, no one ever got around to the specifics. My sex education came primarily from sitting around with groups of other teenage boys and listening to their stories. This information was often grossly exaggerated and, sometimes, completely inaccurate. Other teachers about sex were the girls I dated. However, they seemed to know less than I did or were afraid to admit that they knew more out of concern for their reputation. My dad was responsible for my primary parenting after mother died. He offered very little sex education except to say that, "five minutes of pleasure can bring a lifetime of regret," apparently referring to the pitfalls of careless sexual pleasure.

Since the basics were not discussed, it follows that there was also little guidance in the area of intimacy and its relationship to spirituality. I wonder if my dad taught me more about avoiding intimacy than how to experience it. I was exposed to religion, but didn't know much about spirituality. In any case, I still use "birds and bees," not as a code but as an analogy in discussing spirituality, sexuality, and intimacy. In my early sixties now, I have both information and direct experience with these three topics. I am comfortable with the subject. However, I am still learning. I also have direct experience with the birds and the bees, being a lover of nature. I learned much about intimacy and its relationship to spirituality through my contact with nature: plant, animal, and human. In the space that follows, you will get another story and find information I gathered along the way. If it speaks to you, use it as you wish. Departing from adherence to a traditional silence on the subject, this story includes general, symbolic, and specific issues that relate to spirituality, sexuality, and intimacy.

The birds: Callings of the mourning dove

A few years ago while actively grieving my mother's death; I began to associate the sound of the mourning dove with her memory. It was a pleasant association that helped me connect with the sad and forlorn feelings of loss. These birds also helped me feel a renewed sense of connectedness to and intimacy with my mother and Mother Earth, in general. Both symbolized tender intimacy, gentle love, and birthing of new life to me. For these reasons, I chose the mourning dove as the bird that helps illustrate the many opportunities for intimacy in all relations. To learn about sexuality and intimacy from these birds, I learned the Native American practice of looking closely at their habits and applying their lessons to daily life. Through Native American spirituality and the symbolism, I tapped into a spiritual river of universal truths that connects a specific life event to deeper ways of making meaning out of suffering.

Natural Connections

Even today, close observation of animal life in their natural setting provides us with a wealth of information that can be applied to human life. Short of actual observation, we can research and find reports on the internet from people who have been there. Consider the following similarities and see if they apply to your life situation.

Doves call out to each other. The mourning dove got its name from the sad cooing sound made by the male. It reminded me of the cooing sounds often made between infants and their mothers. These calls remind us that some of our earliest, most basic means of communication are simple, yet vitally important in our total journey through this life.

Doves are inclusive. Many doves live in flocks that include more than one species. The considerable number of birds in a flock increases the chance of finding food and provides protection against such enemies as cats, hawks, martens, owls, and rats. Blackbirds and sparrows often join flocks of doves which further improve the chances of locating food and of being warned of danger. In this way, the mourning dove calls us to honor inclusiveness. It enhances protection and survival.

This runs contrary to the idea of rugged individualism that suggests people must isolate and suffer alone. It also counters the survivalist attitude that suggests the need to keep people from getting too close.

As a child, I learned to use separateness as protection. Over time, this isolation gave birth to more pain, a terrible loneliness that left me feeling set apart from the rest of the family, from the rest of humanity. I divided the world into two parts: "me" and everyone else. The following false beliefs became dominant: "no one else can share my pain so it must be mine alone;" "there is no one like me;" "there will be no one for me;" "I must depend on myself."

With the global problems facing this planet, new voices are surfacing. They call for collective action and a greater sensitivity to how other people's problems ultimately have a negative impact on everyone. Therefore, the mourning dove calls all people to seek intimacy and join forces in searching for solutions to the problems of isolation, hunger, and aggression across the planet.

Doves are committed. They mate for life, while many other kinds of birds mate with different partners. Mourning doves use a ritualistic courtship that begins in the air and finishes on the ground with a series of rhythmic coos and calls. This is called "billing and cooing." The breeding season follows courtship and starts early. Therefore, a pair of doves may rear three or even four broods in a year with both partners sharing the chores of nest building and incubation.

These habits are instructive. First, they invite people to realize the wisdom of careful consideration for our choices of sexual partners. Second, commitment to another person is important in relationships. These habits also highlight the importance of fathers sharing duties in the home and developing close relationships with their children.

Doves make connections. With whistling wing beats, flocks of ashy, slender-necked doves fly across Mother Earth in the spring. These trusting migrants seem to put down anywhere. They appear by a water hole in the desert, by a dirt road in the Corn Belt, in a barnyard to feed with the poultry, drink with the cattle, and even at bird feeders in the city. Like other members of the bird family, the mourning dove needs plenty of water to help soften its dry, hard food. Travelers throughout history have welcomed the sight of this bird as a sign of connectedness between land and water.

Shamans are connectors. Love is the connecting energy. Shamans remind us that we are all connected to nature, each other, and to the universe. This helps us remember that we are never alone. Remembering this helps us to make connections in a meaningful way, especially when suffering.

With these lessons, we can make connections between various events of our lives, learn to follow the sound of God's gentle whisper, and attend to signs or coincidences that offer guidance. An example of this involves looking to the subconscious to illuminate and direct the conscious mind by journaling our nightly dreams. The dove calls us to seek connections between the seen and unseen realities of life. Through these various connections you fix your eyes on an eternal glory that far outweighs your momentary troubles.

Doves are prosperous. The mourning dove does not fear humankind and has even prospered from our mistreatment of Mother Earth. For example, land mismanagement caused by overgrazing and poor conservation practices results in soil erosion. Doves seem to benefit because of the resulting growth of weeds that produce seeds for food. In this way, doves direct us to look for the advantages in disadvantageous situations.

In my childhood, it was a very disadvantageous situation when mother died leaving my dad with an infant child and six other children. The details of this situation raise questions of relationship mismanagement. The advantage that I realized from this tragic event was that I could overcome the apparent pain of separation and loss of intimacy caused by mother's death. I learned to grieve. This led me to forgiveness. By forgiving the hurts, I could move on with my life. Later, I developed a personal sense of connectedness with mother that transcends this physical world. In this way I prospered from my mother's death. I learned to forgive and expand my sense of connectedness. I experienced spiritual growth.

Forgiveness is an important aspect of relationship management and spiritual growth. This requires a tremendous amount of work. It is difficult to pardon someone who has never been on trial. This is why it is important to gather evidence, examine our memories of past hurts, and understand how the past still affects us today. Releasing emotions, such as anger and hurt, is beneficial when done constructively. When possible, gently confront your persecutors in person and tell them how you were hurt. This sets the stage for forgiveness to begin. Reconciliation often follows forgiveness as the process is completed.

Spiritual Connections

Doves are important symbols in many spiritual disciplines. Native Americans believed that when the mourning dove called out and its answer was not returned, then it called for you. Most often doves symbolically call us toward peace and give us hope. In addition, doves symbolize the interconnectedness between the seen and unseen worlds. If the sound of the mourning dove appeals to you, consider the nature of your personal calling, your life's mission. We are all called as ministers and your spiritual gifts give life to your ministry.

Knowing and following your mission is a spiritual gift that you both receive and give. It involves following the inner voice of your soul and determining which gifts you received at your spiritual birth. It connects to the essence of who you are, your inner child. It represents your deepest intention. Mission is the overall journey of your soul in this life.

Once you understand that you have a calling, then you can connect who you are to what you do. It does not mean you have to change your job or mate, but you change the way you relate. It gives more meaning to your daily activities. This is a challenge faced by everyone every day of our lives: to squeeze a purpose out of the sameness of each day.

Callings are both vertical and horizontal. Therefore, remember to look upward as well as across the breakfast table when considering your life's mission. It does not have to be grandiose. Neither is it to be feared. Many are called to humbly and simply love with an open heart. God's perfect love drives out fear, so fix your mind on love. Consider how the dove relates to your spiritual mission.

The ascending dove points upward. This symbol reminds us to live in the spirit of the resurrection, not the shadow of the crucifixion. It gently calls us to work steadfastly toward fulfilling our higher purpose: living in the spirit of innocence, peace, forgiveness, gentleness, self-control, and love of life. It also reminds us to find ways to honor our Higher Power, who many call God, while working through pain and suffering. This involves looking for the advantages within our disadvantages, as I did in my personal grief work. Find ways to connect a positive with the negative in this life and offer them both up for higher purposes. This can be an uplifting experience.

The descending dove points downward. It reminds us to acknowledge the eternal presence of a loving Creator who responds with heartfelt caring when we silently call for help. This Loving Spirit awaits our call for help as an invitation to descend from the heavens and wipe the tears from our eyes. It also calls us to reconsider our connectedness with loved ones who have gone on to the unseen world. When we allow a continued connection with lost loved ones, then we can recognize and honor signs as communications from the unseen world. These relationships do not end. They change and continue spiritually, as the old order of things pass away.

Native Americans also believed that if someone dies and does not have anyone in the entire world to remember him and cry for him, the mourning dove remembers and mourns for him. Therefore, if we remember someone we loved that died, and then the mourning dove would not have to mourn for him. So, when you hear the mourning dove, remember your lost loved ones and the dove will not sound so lonesome. This helps us remember that we are never alone because of our connection to nature and the unseen world.

Musical Connections

There is more to the story. It was through my appreciation of the Native American traditions and Southwestern art that I developed an interest in Native American flute music. I soon noticed a similarity between the cooing sound of the male mourning dove and the sounds of the flute. I thought of the flute when I heard the doves and of the doves when I heard the flute. The association was so strong that to think of one was to think of the other.

The flute, an ancient instrument, may have been a mechanical reproduction of the dove's call. They have other similarities. Flutes were used by Native Americans for courting rituals. Doves also have established rituals for courting. An Indian brave created original music to tell some girl he was interested in her, or that he waited for her, or that he missed her. This courtship often led to marriage. When he died, his music and his flute were buried with him.

Think of your life mission as the melody of a flute, the theme of your life. Career, on the other hand, can be compared to the flute itself, the instrument you play the melody on. You can express your mission in varying and interesting ways, but the melody stays the same. In this way, the flute reminds us that our life's mission can offer a constant melody as background music in our daily activities. It also reminds us that there are many other musical instruments through which a person can express their life's mission.

The flute is only an instrument, a tool. It requires a person skillfully breathing through it to make the magic we call "music." The flute serves as a channel, a conduit, through which the magic of music can be made. I recorded the following dream that helps illustrate the magical nature of the flute:

> *I am riding in a wagon with my older brother. Tied to the wagon and following along beside it is a young bull calf wounded and crippled by a deep cut. Obviously from registered stock, this buff-colored calf is almost like a pet because it had been raised for showing in contests. But now it will be slaughtered because of the injury. My brother seems happy, despite the situation.*

> *Then my brother brings out a brass musical instrument like I had never seen. It is rounded and blunt with two pieces that appear perfectly machined to fit together. The mouthpiece can be reversed, but only plays when placed in the proper way, creating a channel through which the breath flows. He cannot make music on it as he attempts to play "taps" for the bull.*

> *I take the flute and begin to play it very easily. The sound is like pan pipes, a very special, soft sound of the flute. As I play, I glimpse visions of the Kingdom of Heaven, which disappear when I quit playing. As I play again and experiment with it, I become more proficient and experience the Kingdom each time I play. I talk to other people about the special nature of the flute and they show interest, but act as if they do not believe me.*

> *While my brother found this brass instrument somewhere in the pasture,*

I know that I am meant to play it. I get a sense that it is very special and need to
protect it or someone will steal it. It makes sounds with magical qualities that create
visions of heaven. I then awaken from the dream.

The dream helped me realize how I open to the spirit through music. On another level, the flute in this dream represents humankind, who can serve as a channel, an instrument through which God can blow His breath. In this sense, we are called to serve as a conduit of God: His living flute.

God created humankind in his image and then humans returned the compliment. Therefore, we must be careful with the idea of a Higher Power "as we understand Him." It is far too easy to create our own idea of God from the dark corners of our selfish ego. We must rely on a combination of standard readings (such as the Bible and other religious materials), authorities on the subject, and our individual discernment. When we do, the result can be music, and we become a conduit to higher realities.

Music opens the doors of our hearts and spirits to the Kingdom of Heaven. Therefore, the song of the mourning dove, nature's music, can gently remind us that we are all called to a higher mission: to love and minister unto one another. This provides direction to look more closely at doves, their habits and mannerisms, for individual guidance.

Callings for Consideration

If you relate to the descriptions of the mourning dove, consider the following questions:

1) Are you responding to your life's calling?

2) Have you been following someone else's idea of what you are "supposed" to do?

3) Do you have difficulty asking for help, including asking God for help in specific life situations?

4) How do you call for attention? What rituals do you use to attract others to you? Are these self-destructive methods?

The mourning dove can appear indirectly, such as through a growing appreciation for the sound of the flute or another musical instrument. If this happens, we might consider how we have been ignoring various callings. For example, have we been ignoring our body's call for rest, relaxation, or exercise? If recurring illness or chronic fatigue plagues you, then maybe your body is calling on you for better treatment. The mourning dove calls us from intellectual pursuits to attend to matters of the heart, body and soul. The dove calls us to reconsider our priorities.

Consider the following additional questions:

1) Who would you call out to if on your deathbed?

2) Have you elevated work or another relationship in your life to a point of worship?

3) Are you putting someone else in your life before you, to the point of self-neglect?

4) Maybe you have some unresolved grief issues to deal with. Have you suffered recent losses through which you have not taken the time to grieve?

5) Have you been lonely and feeling unloved?

Most people's behavior can be interpreted as either expressing love or calling for love. Perhaps you are being called out of your self-imposed prison and isolation toward relationships, companionship, and intimacy. If so, you can be sure that the Spirit also calls.

Sooner or later, we must realize that isolation provides safety and protection, but also cages and imprisons the part of us that is most precious and loving. This self-imposed prison cuts us off from a major source of love and a sense of belonging to the greater good in the universe that provides eternal protection.

The bees: Callings of the honeybee

I was a beekeeper for fourteen years. It was during my younger days, not as I grew older, like some people. During this time, I managed from one to twenty hives of bees. It was a fascinating enterprise that involved hard, sweaty work during the summer months when hives had to be checked, moved, or harvested. The fresh, golden honey offered rewards well beyond the investment of labor. In the winter months, this gentle craft offered a wealth of intellectual stimulation through reading the research materials that attempted to explain the behavior of these untamed, industrious creatures. It was in this context that I became aware of the ancient symbolism associated with these tiny creatures. I drew from this background and used honeybees to further my lessons on spirituality, sexuality, and intimacy.

Natural Connections

There are many things I learned about human nature by reading about and working with honeybees. The following popular quotation by Tolstoy served as an important first lesson:

> *The trouble begins because men sometimes think that you can handle people without love, and you cannot. You can handle things without love. You can carve wood and hammer iron without it, but you cannot deal with people in this fashion. People are like bees. If you handle bees roughly, either they will get hurt or you will get hurt.*

Perhaps we are much more like bees than we want to admit. Our hurts in relationships are often caused by inconsiderate and unloving actions. Honeybees are like us in many ways, both having positive and negative traits. Consider the similarities.

Honeybees are aggressive. The killer bees (Africanized bees) have put fear in the hearts of people living in the southwestern United States as they have migrated upward from Central America. Paradoxically, Europeans bred honeybees to be relatively gentle, but are less productive. The African honeybee is more productive, but aggressive. Experts soothed our fears of these killer bees. They predicted the aggressiveness would be bred out through mixed breeding with gentler strains before the bees migrate to more populated sections of the United States. Mixed breeding resulted in what became known as, 'hot hives,' a hybrid mix that retained a more aggressive nature. We can be gentle or aggressive. Like the honeybee or the wolf, we have stingers and sharp fangs to use in self-defense. The honeybee instructs us to love the whole self, even the part that makes a stinging remark occasionally. We differ from the honeybee because we sometimes behave aggressively or abusively for reasons other than self-defense.

Honeybees are temperamental. In fair weather I could take the hive apart and the bees would ignore me for the most part. On stormy days I would drive near the beehives and they would go out of their way to sting me. Similarly, we go out of our way to hurt the ones we love most when in a bad mood. Like abuse, there is a reason for inconsideration and moodiness. It is part of our nature. By allowing it and owning up to it, you can watch it and keep it in check. Remember, gentleness gets angry too. When we see rough feelings as a part of our nature, we can develop an ability to show strength without the need for hurtful words or actions. The greatest strength is shown through kindness and compassion as we forgive each other.

Honeybees are resilient. The honeybee's natural enemy is the wax worm. The eggs and larvae of the enemy are always present in the beehive. However, the only time wax worms present a threat is when the hive's population weakens.

In many ways, our physiological, psychological, and spiritual immune systems work like this. We live in the presence of threats to our emotional and

~ 47 ~

physical health. If we maintain a strong immunity, then neither disease, nor dysfunction, nor evil presents a serious threat. But when our immune system is permanently weakened, we suffer the slow process of dying from the inside out. We regress into old unhealthy habits, diseased survival mechanisms that are self-destructive.

Honeybees are industrious. This is reflected in their collective efforts in gathering life's necessities for survival and in fiercely protecting themselves from being preyed upon. In this way, they symbolically advocate the practice of being industrious to all creatures.

Be careful to avoid excessive industry. Excessive behaviors are usually self-defeating and have a negative effect on relationships, impacting both sexuality and intimacy. As children, some people learned to earn their place and sense of worth. They became human "doings" with a performance-based sense of worth. They learned to guess where their place was, learned to be thankful for being allowed to stay, and became excessively accommodating. Others became workaholics who neglect self, partners, and children in favor of career, accomplishments, and competition.

With these things in mind, the industriousness of the honeybee teaches us several things. First, we must avoid the extremes of industry: either becoming excessive doers or being complacent while our fellow creatures are in need. Second, we must accept responsibility for getting our goals and desires met cooperatively. Finally, we must learn to relate to others neither as predator nor as victim through increased understanding of self and others.

Honeybees are mutually dependent. Each member of the swarm has a specific role. Together they work for the common good, feeding the larvae, gathering and storing nectar and pollen, and cleaning house. When we survey nature, we see humankind in infancy and childhood being more helpless than most creatures. Humans lie languishing for days and months. Infants are totally incapable of self-sufficiency, defenseless against predators, unable to provide shelter from extreme weather, or even to provide for their nourishment. In most developed countries, children are dependent on their parents, especially their mothers, for survival during these early years.

Sex and intimacy in a marriage often suffers during birthing and child rearing years because the child is put before the relationship. This practice suggests that it is both natural and necessary to be dependent as an infant, but adults must keep their priorities in mind. In adult relationships interdependence and shared parenting works best. Keeping the marriage as a top priority also helps prevent loss of intimacy.

It might have pleased the Creator to have made humans the most dependent creatures because dependence bonds us to society, nature, and Mother Earth. Humans are dependent upon each other for protection and security. In infancy, children learn the importance of depending on parents for survival. In return, grown adult children lovingly provide support for their parents, children, and other significant relatives in their lives. Increasingly, other life forms and, Mother Earth herself, are becoming dependent upon humans for protection and preservation. The honeybee symbolically calls us to a life of service; the noblest part of the work of the Kingdom. To do less, we may be deemed a drone in the hive of nature, a useless member of society.

Honeybees are obedient. In Hebrew the name of the bee signifies "to administer, to govern, to put in order," or "to act like a swarm of bees." The honeybee is one of few creatures that has a feminine monarch for a ruler. Individual bees work together cooperatively under her rule for the good of the swarm. The honeybee, therefore, stands as a symbol of royalty, sacred inspiration, and obedience.

Honeybees are wise. They gather nectar and collectively condense it into honey by evaporating the moisture with their wings. Honey represents wisdom, which relates to characteristics of an effective leader. Wisdom is as sweet to the soul as honey is to the taste. In looking at the regulated labor of these insects, it is easy to view them as an emblem of wisdom, obedience, and systematic industry. Therefore, the honeybee calls us to value cooperative leadership in relationships and to honor the best of masculine and feminine leadership qualities.

Most relationships involve power or control issues. These must be resolved to enhance intimacy. Masochism and sadism sometimes surface when control issues polarize. Masochism is sadism in disguise, self-hatred. These kinds of relationships are more into hating than for mutual need fulfillment. It's easy to get into blaming in situations where we have been hurt or abused. Words like, "look how they screwed me up," often are spoken. An effective way to hate and hold onto your anger is to stay screwed up and blame your parents or your current or ex-spouse. Problems with other authority figures often surface too. The solution is to take control of yourself and accept responsibility for your present situation. In this way you become empowered, knowing when to stand and when to yield. Trust your Higher Power and wisdom will guide you to know when.

Honeybees are full of surprises. A keeper of honeybees, like anyone who has yielded to the cycles and patterns of nature, can always turn to these tiny creatures. They are untamed, but seem to profit from domestic management of hives. While a large body of research exists about bees, they still have a perpetual store of surprises. Paradoxically, they also have a mysterious constancy beneath this unpredictability. Therefore, the honeybee can direct us to an enterprise that provides a constant and unfailing source of curiosity, enjoyment, and happiness. In this sense, we are directed to value the elements of constancy and surprise in relationships.

We are all the creation of the same Higher Power and share this lovely earth with a multitude of life forms, great and small. People are not on this good earth to dominate her, to seduce her, or exploit her. She is not a warehouse or dumping ground placed at our disposal for our exclusive benefit. We are here to make Mother Earth our home, to share her, to glorify her, and to glorify our Creator.

Callings for Consideration

If the honeybee has swarmed its way in your life today, you may want to consider the following individual questions:

1) How well have you been regulating your sense of industry? Have you overstepped your boundaries in pursuit of career and purpose, neglecting those who are dependent on you?

2) Are you avoiding facing your dependency issues?

3) Have you been acting as a "keeper of the earth" or exploiting her?

4) How well do you protect yourself from exploitation?

If the honeybee has appeared to you in some indirect manner, it may be instructing you to avoid complacency and helplessness. Otherwise, you may become drone-like. Drones contribute little to a hive, except housekeeping duties and a rare chance to mate with the queen. They are noisy and never sting anybody because they have no stinger. Consequently, people knowledgeable about honeybees easily recognize drones and never pay any attention to their noise. Have people been ignoring you or not taking you seriously?

At the other extreme, you may want to consider if you have been compulsively independent. You may have developed an aversion to dependency and have difficulty with intimacy, becoming uncomfortable if someone gets too close.

In pursuing independence, you may have developed a pattern of indiscriminate sexual behavior. Learn another lesson from the drone. While mating with the virgin queen in mid-air he explodes with a loud pop and then, almost as quickly, falls backward and downward from the sky, paralyzed. He often leaves his genitalia in the queen as he falls to his death. Similarly, sex without commitment takes a part of us away when our partner leaves. Have you become inconsiderate of yourself and others in your quest for independence and sexual pleasure? Consider this if you want to prevent unwanted consequences.

Perhaps this is a time in your life to commit to a period of abstinence from sexual involvement. This could pave the way to learn how to be intimate in relationships. Passionate people, like nuns and monks, choose chastity. Celibacy is another form of abstinence that people can choose. Abstinence is a healthy choice especially when sexual urges have become self-defeating and dysfunctional. Other valid reasons some people practice sexual abstinence are:

1) Sex complicates relationships;

2) They do not want to be distracted from the love of God; and

3) To reduce risks of pregnancies or contracting sexually transmitted diseases.

With the widespread application of 12-step programs to social issues, the general idea of abstinence has become more popular. Sexual abstinence has gained popularity with the explosion of social problems, such as AIDS, hepatitis C, teenage pregnancies, and abortions. Remember, risks for health problems increase by engaging in sexual behavior indiscriminately even though a person's lips may seem to drip with honey. These social problems not only call for abstinence in some circumstances, but highlight the importance of commitment with intimacy in all relationships.

The human: Callings to intimacy & spirituality

The biblical description of the Garden of Eden creates visions of a natural utopia. All creatures lived in communion with God and each other. They had nothing to hide.

In many ways, we experience a similar bond with our environment as an infant. During childhood, we encounter the snakes of life and eat of the forbidden fruit. We call this childhood trauma and neglect. In this manner, we recreate the drama of the Garden of Eden.

Barriers to Intimacy

Childhood hurts rob us of innocence, thrusts us into self-consciousness, leaving us feeling isolated and exposed. In response to these real and imagined threats, we become defensive. We go into hiding in order to survive. Protective coping habits develop during childhood and adolescence that often endure throughout a lifetime. Our task is to transform those primitive defenses into more mature ones and regain that sense of unity, peace, openness, and intimacy with all life.

Hidden defenses from past hurts act as natural barriers to intimacy. For example, bad relationships with parents leave self-defeating beliefs such as, "it will never work out for me." However, we trudge ahead and give it a try anyway, looking for the new relationship to change the reality of the past. When this does not work, we form additional self-defeating beliefs such as, "all relationships hurt." This type of thinking is one-dimensional, myopic. At this point, we do not know what to do except to retreat or blame the problems on somebody else.

Soon our beliefs and attitudes begin producing the reality of our present experiences. For example, the experience of being loved brings new problems to the surface. We develop unrealistic expectations from beliefs such as, "you should make me whole, caring and loving." The belief that says, "the next relationship will make up for the hurt and pain of the past ones" keep us searching. At this point, we begin putting up boundaries for protection.

Whatever we feel, however deeply we feel it, most of us learn to camouflage our true emotions. We show the world only what we imagine will be acceptable and keep the rest secret and hidden. Thus, no one really knows us, no one really sees us, and no one really hears us. Even if people love us, they love us for what we pretend to be. Later, we find that the biggest boundary is the wall we build around us that separates, divides, and inhibits intimacy.

We divide the world into two groups: those who are good enough and those who are not. This is a two-dimensional, dichotomous, level of truth that blocks us from love and intimacy. We hide behind a wall that protects and alienates us from others. We fear being discovered. We hide a secret belief that we are among the ones who are not good enough.

Our basic belief about reality must be changed to higher levels before relationships can get better. We must come to believe that we are all of equal worth, precious children of the universe. We are neither 'special' nor 'nobody,' but simply 'nobody special,' equally worthwhile. Higher levels of reality help us feel totally available to loved ones, including lost loved ones albeit spiritually. These higher dimensions of reality help us to feel connected in many places and with many people simultaneously, like a computer hacker surfing on the information superhighway, except with more heart and soul. Therefore, our experiences in all our relations are an individual responsibility. When our beliefs change, only then can our experiences change.

To move from a two-dimensional framework of reality, we must move from contradictions that deal with the idea of sacrificing everything for the one and only. Another contradiction to be abandoned is the one that suggests we have to love and be intimate with everyone or be intimate with no one. At this stage, people have two contradictory fears: of being close and of being alone. We are called to love humanly, which is imperfect, and to love with wholeness, which is unconditional. This means loving ourselves and others unconditionally, including the ones who are difficult to love. This opens the way to consider useful questions such as, "is this one for me?" and "will this work for me?" It also eliminates fear-based questions such as, "if I can't guarantee it will work, then why bother to try?" We come to realize that relationships are conditional, but, with God's help, we can love unconditionally. At this point, we are shifting into higher dimensions of reality.

To achieve intimacy, we must seek these higher realities. Higher truths are unifying. They include wholeness. They also direct us to recognize our incompleteness. We must both claim personal power and acknowledge our weaknesses. We must strive for both individuation and interdependence. In this way, we discover a higher way of being that integrates contradictory parts of our personality without polarities or limits. Only by working toward being our best selves can we enjoy a balanced relationship.

The ideal of rugged individualism is a social script that has caused much interpersonal damage. It encourages us to fake it by hiding our weaknesses and failures. It contributes to shame for having limitations. It pushes us to pretend and act as if we were without needs and are in total control of our lives. It leads to keeping up appearances and concern for image. Finally, it isolates us socially. Underneath, this behavior often hides a fundamental feeling of being "flawed." In reaction, we put on acts, like a "John Wayne" act. This rugged individualism leads to arrogance.

We look at each other through "hard eyes," like a cornered animal. Soft individualism affirms our imperfections and leads to humility. In this way, we can look at each other through "soft eyes" with love and compassion. So, dare to share more of your humbleness, your deeper thoughts and your personal life story. Avoid trying to appear to have it together in a certain stereotypical way.

True intimacy involves one person willing to be truly himself in the presence of another person willing to be truly herself. We cannot truly be ourselves until we can share freely the things we most have in common. Examples of these include our weaknesses, our incompleteness, our imperfections, our inadequacies, our sins, and our lack of wholeness and self-sufficiency. This is how intimacy becomes spiritual. We provide compassion and comfort to each other as we have received it from God. It helps connect us together.

Steps to Intimacy

Take the following individual steps for more intimate and loving relationships:

STEP 1: Do your homework. Educate yourself about intimacy. Read about it. Talk about it with your significant other. Define intimacy so you'll know it when you experience it. Do the same with love. Believe that you are never alone. Identify what stands in the way of intimacy. Realize that you are most often propelled into isolation by fear, sadness, or hurt. Your irrational assumption is that if you withdraw from everyone else, you can make the painful, uncomfortable feelings go away. Rather than hide, your challenge is to speak what is true, to share the tender contents of your heart, to describe for others the emotional geography of your deepest concerns. When you name your feelings truthfully, first to yourself, then to others, you invite a rush of sympathetic vibration from those who are suddenly free to enter your life. They become allies. They can love and touch and share your deepest hurts.

Discover the masculine voice of intimacy and learn how to understand it. A masculine energy favors side-by-side interaction. Intimacy is expressed through "doing" interactions rather than by "being" interactions. It involves our intellect, our thinking and sensing functions. It is primarily concerned with survival. Support is sometimes expressed by providing real help in a crisis or giving people privacy. Self-disclosure is usually limited to strengths while weaknesses are concealed. Emotions and desires are often expressed through anger or concealed humor. Underneath this humor you find anger, hurt, and desire.

The feminine voice of intimacy is from the heart, involving our feelings and intuition. It is concerned with our spirit. Men often fall in love with a woman to reconnect with his inner heart function. He sees her as a mirror of his spiritual self.

STEP 2: Admit your secrets to yourself. This cuts out adolescent-like performance-based sharing, like trying to see who had the most traumatic childhood. Look in the mirror and tell yourself your secrets, honestly. Then turn your secrets into controllable behaviors. You are only as well as your secrets.

Practice speaking the truth. Seek to understand your truth at higher levels. Learning to speak the truth with clarity and courage is a potent doorway to intimate community and relationships with others. Begin by choosing one person, such as a close friend, a lover, a spouse, anyone who you are willing to trust. Ask them to sit with you for ten minutes and just listen in silence to what you have to say. At the end of ten minutes, ask your friend to summarize what he has heard. As you become more comfortable, expand your practice of speaking what is true with other friends.

STEP 3: Start doing the action of intimacy. This involves responding, respecting, and caring for the purpose of providing tenderness. Start giving security, trust, love, and understanding.

You may also use your own pain to make contact with the simultaneous suffering of all other beings. You may begin by allowing the image of someone close to you, who you care for deeply, and allow yourself to become aware of their pain, places in their lives where they have felt sadness, hurt, or loss. Feel how their pain is a mirror of the sorrows you carry within yourself. Feel how the pain connects you; also feel how, touching this pain while being attentive opens a door to mutual love and intimacy.

Practice daily. Correct practice is the key.

STEP 4: Give yourself permission to be successful. Learn to let love in. Affirm, "I now give myself permission to be intimate and successful in having loving relationships in my life." Allow more intimacy in your life. Remember, sex is often taken as intimacy, but if rushed or engaged in without commitment, it is only a poor substitute for love and intimacy. Intimacy comes together after building trust, taking risks, and making commitments that are mutually agreed upon. In this context, sex comes as an extension of intimacy. This takes time. So, take your time!

STEP 5: Admit to yourself that you have impact. Declare it, and insist that you will have intimacy. To admit that you have impact means you share responsibility for hurt or love in relationships. Give yourself the gift of admitting that you have impact. When you admit responsibility for your problems, you have the power to find solutions. Be proactive instead of reactive. You create impact, whether you believe it or not. Say to the world, "Wake up everybody, I'm letting love in!"

STEP 6: Evaluate where you are on the following levels of intimacy:
- with your Higher Power and ideals, such as truth and honesty;
- with self, including your inner friends, such as your inner child, higher self, and other parts of the personality;
- with your partner or spouse;
- with your family;
- with your occupation; and
- with animals, plants, and things.

STEP 7: Stretch your self-image. Do not take your childhood so seriously. Let go of your trauma-based identity. Imagine that what happened to you was simply something that happened to a precious child of God. Remember no particular reason other than it happened, and it was very sad, and it hurt deeply. Come to believe that your suffering was not unique, but it happens in some way to all God's children. This is what connects us together. Most of all, remember the positive lessons gleaned from your suffering. This gives it meaning.

It has been said that reality follows image, so stretch your self-image. Make it grow and expand.

STEP 8: Stop testing life and start celebrating it! You are not here to be understood. You are here to be understanding. Start opening to the celebration of life. Practice it as a spiritual discipline.

Decide to let it be all right for you and your partner to let love in and to adjust to the cycles of getting close and getting more independent.

Cycles of Intimacy

The cycles of intimacy can be compared to the rhythm of breathing; with breathing in as closeness and breathing out as separation. Failure to breathe properly in relationships leaves us feeling smothered, breathless, or in need of breathing room. To overcome these problems, we must move from automatic, unconscious patterns of behavior, and like conscious breathing, develop intentional rhythms of moving in and out of intimacy. We must make agreements with our partners regarding intentions in the relationship and live our lives on purpose.

Intimacy is also like a flower that bursts into full bloom and then dies. In a while, another bloom comes along to take its place. During the bloom, we intentionally allow closeness and experience the nectar of intimacy. This involves dealing with whatever occurs to get in the way of intimacy during closeness. It also involves practicing enjoyment of the full pleasure and positive energy of love and closeness. Therefore, sex is best when it flows naturally from intimacy. Then when the bloom fades and falls away, we overcome a tendency to feel lonely and embrace the separateness. This involves seeing yourself as a whole person with a life, standing with assurance, and having other positive relationships.

Earth vibrates something like eighty-eight cycles per minute, like a heartbeat. Shamans are tuned into these vibrations. I imagine the entire universe follows a similar pattern. Love and fear are forms of this vibrational energy that form a composite of sexual energy as they dance together. Love is the energy that stimulates the desire to connect, to join. Being in love enables us to feel connected to the whole universe. Fear is the energy that separates and divides. We are a composite of both energies. This contributes to our life force, our sexuality.

The sexual and spiritual aspects of our being are so close together, that to awaken one is to awaken the other. It is an arousing experience. Spiritual and sexual energies affect the genitals. Self-actualized people have reported experiencing orgasm as a mystical or spiritual event. Over history, nuns and monks have written quality erotic poetry. Therefore, as we grow spiritually, our sexual attractiveness also grows.

Sexual urges often arise out of a sense of incompleteness. It's comparable to an urge to merge and a yearning toward wholeness. Some people attach a sense of reverence to sex, but complications often surface. For some people, sex is the closest they come to God. Conversely, people who complain of sexual problems may have spiritual problems. It is difficult to separate one from the other.

Our number one priority becomes our Higher Power. It can be with God. Most often it is with work or the children. We can see God as a top priority, a seducer luring us to Him. Many people mistakenly search for spirituality through romantic love. They seek to meet that person who will meet all their needs. This is a direct violation of the first commandment admonishing us to put nothing before God. However, it is common to put the romantic partner first during courtship. After marriage, some people change their priorities and neglect the relationship. When we observe a marriage turn sour, it seems there are only two reasons people marry:

1) for production of children; or

2) to create friction, divorce, and move on.

Therefore, after marriage people often go back to putting work or another pursuit before the relationship. When children are born, they often put the kids first. In the case of a remarriage, people will go back to putting their kids or work first. In either case, the relationship suffers when reduced to a low priority status. When the relationship suffers, usually the quality of intimacy and sex also suffers. At its best, marriage is a gateway to spiritual growth.

Sexuality, like marriage, is a natural part of the human experience. It is a powerful force. When channeled within the boundaries of a committed relationship, it can bring joy and be another gateway to spiritual growth. Otherwise, when released without discipline and commitment, it can be a powerful negative force that perpetuates pain and suffering.

When stress and strains restrict the flow of love and affection in a relationship, people will look for substitutes for love. They sometimes look inside the family or outside the family and form unhealthy bonds of affection. If these relations get romantic and sexual outside the marriage, we call this "having an affair." If these excessively close bonds within the family get sexual, we call this "incest." Short of that, we just call it spoiling the child or playing favorites.

When someone betrays us, we often feel superior or entitled to put down the one who betrayed us. We may become cynical and distrusting. Time is essential to the healing of our wounds and betrayals. However, the real trust begins when you decide to trust someone, knowing that betrayal is inevitable when you stay close to someone for a long time. To do this, you must develop a trust in yourself that you can survive the pain of betrayal.

Incest victims tend to have a highly distorted view of God and sexuality. For them love and sacrifice is often most powerfully proven by their willingness not to know. Denial dominates their relationships with others and with God. Pain and sacrifice is what they relate to the most. Therefore, they tend to stay in destructive relationships and tolerate unwanted treatment from their partners.

Even when we know about denial, it is impossible to know completely what we are doing is right. This is because the unconscious mind seems one step ahead of the conscious mind. To master unconscious influences or unhealthy habits, we must stay informed, face reality, practice healthy habits, and maintain awareness in the present moment.

Sex and intimacy can be discussed symbolically or platonically but ultimately gets expressed sensually, in the flesh. Enjoying sexual intimacy requires us to be grounded in our bodies and in the present moment. It also requires the ability to get out of our heads into our hearts. We must relate to our partner with commitment in the spirit of unconditional and eternal love. To practice unconditional love, we must stay close to God. Intimacy with God is like intimacy in marriage. It ebbs and flows. Therefore, we learn to go with the flow, to move in and out of the cycles of intimacy. In learning these skills, we can bring higher levels of reality into this life that contains more love and wisdom. As you open to these realities, keep seeking guidance from your best self, the part of yourself that knows how to keep doing it. In this way, you can keep love alive until you experience the ultimate intimacy: complete union with your Creator.

The story concludes. I found a way to decode "birds and bees" that enlightened and guided me toward my life's mission, my calling. I also made sense out of the expression, "five minutes of pleasure can bring a lifetime of regret." On one level, it was the instruction of a father to his son. On another level, it was the father's coded expression of grief and guilt.

Yet on a greater, human level this expression refers to solutions to the world's problems of population management, sexual exploitation, and epidemics of disease. Sexual behavior is causing people to die in many ways, such as through AIDS, Hepatitis C, and abortion. When managed with a sense of commitment, responsibility, and intimacy, sex both creates life and enhances life. Practice the lessons of the father, the birds, and the bees, by keeping your passions within the bounds of love and commitment.

Notes

CHAPTER 3

ADOPTING: HOW TO TAKE CARE OF YOURSELF

Orphaned, that's what I felt like. My father had died leaving me feeling alone and on my own. I had grown up in a family of seven children. My father raised six of them at home, partly as a single parent. My mother had died when I was still a child. I was a teenager when my father died. A paternal aunt and uncle raised my youngest brother whom they adopted after daddy died. Too old for adoption, I was on my own. After a couple of years in limbo and grief, I married to begin a family.

I was the fifth child. At times, I felt neglected or ignored by my dad. I didn't have the words for it back then. That was just the way it was. The neglect was, in part, due to being one child in a large family with other children demanding my father's attention. Another part was because daddy stayed busy working, sometimes on two jobs. I learned very early that I had to look after myself, coming to unconsciously believe that I could only depend on myself. However, I really didn't learn much about taking loving care of myself because I was mostly uninformed and inexperienced on this subject.

Depending upon life experiences, everyone has the benefit of parenting. Supporting the child in his uniqueness and providing love and structure is what parenting is about, ideally. You may have received some version of this from your biological parents or from other caregivers. We tend to parent our children like the way we were parented. In certain cases where there was an obvious negative example, many adults swear to avoid the pattern and consciously parent their children in diverse ways. We attempt to avoid the parenting mistakes of our ancestors, but many of these patterns come through anyway. A chill often comes over us as we find ourselves blurting out some outrageous remark that suddenly sounds very much like the voice of our mother or father. The effects of parenting are long-lasting and filter down from generation to generation, unless a conscious change is made.

Our parenting experiences also become a part of our personality and we treat ourselves much like our parents treated us. Therefore, if a parent was critical, we become self-critical and have difficulty with self-acceptance. If a parent was abusive, we become self-abusive or wander from one abusive relationship to another. If a parent was pre-occupied and neglectful, we tend to preoccupy our minds and neglect our health emotionally, physically, or spiritually. To overcome these errors, we must become conscious of our self-defeating patterns and learn to parent ourselves better.

Consider the idea of adopting yourself. This idea comes from the many people whose lives have been touched by adoption in some manner. These are the people who gave up children for adoption, who have adopted children, or who have been adopted themselves. Ecologists and animal rights activists have extended the idea of adoption to domestic animals and wildlife. This represents an effort to raise funds and bond humans with animals in one family. Now is the time to come full circle and extend the idea of adoption to yourself.

The idea also relates to my feelings of being orphaned and my youngest brother who was adopted by my paternal aunt and uncle. It also relates to anyone who has secretly sought someone to adopt them. This implies they either felt lost and alone, like an orphan, or never felt wanted by their biological parents. Many of these lost ones have gone from relationship to relationship seeking adoption and only getting foster care.

Technically, my youngest brother was placed in the temporary care of the aunt at first. What else could a grieving widower do with a newborn child under those circumstances?

Foster care is a temporary arrangement, usually made by a child-welfare agency. In such an arrangement, the agency places a child, usually from a neglectful, abusive, or poverty-stricken home, in the temporary care of a foster parent. The key word here is temporary. Maybe it's time you ceased trying to place yourself in someone else's temporary care and adopt yourself permanently. If you want continuity and care in your life, then adoption may be the option. It is a choice. Let's explore what this would mean.

Literally, adoption is the legal process whereby a person who is not a child's natural parent chooses to become the child's parent. Once adopted, the child has all the rights and duties of a natural child. Inherent in this process is the giving up of parental rights by the birth parents. What an act of love it must be to give up parental rights. An equal act of love involves taking on parental care of a child you didn't conceive.

Each time my father attempted to regain custody of my brother, my aunt reportedly refused to release him. She had become attached to my brother, being childless herself. Finally, they went to court with a dispute over custody.

Like other legal processes in our society, ancient Roman law has had considerable influence in shaping the adoptive process. For example, in Roman law, an adopted child had the same rights and privileges as a biological child, even if he had been a slave. Whatever the circumstances of the family-of-origin, the adopted child lost all rights in his old family and gained all the rights of a legitimate child in his new family. It was an "either-or" choice. The child was not a second-class member of the new family; he was equal to all other children, biological or adopted, in his new parent's family. He became a full heir to his new father's estate.

My dad refused to give up parental rights and filed for custody. His sister refused to give up my little brother and counter-filed for adoption. Other family members were drawn into the dispute, taking sides.

Actual adoptions may be arranged privately or with the assistance of an agency. The agency investigates both the child's biological parentage and the suitability of the adoptive parent(s). Placements are then reviewed and normally sanctioned by a court, which then issues a new birth certificate designating the adoptive parents as the new parents.

Accusations and hurtful words were spoken regarding the suitability of parenting on opposing sides. In the end, no one got what they wanted. The judge left my brother in our aunt's custody, but refused her petition for adoption.

In the past, most U.S. States required the sealing of agency records from the adoptive family, the child, and the natural parents. The origins for this "either-or" approach probably came from Roman law. The prevailing belief that it was in everyone's best interests to sever connections has survived until recently. Under pressure from adoptive persons wishing to know their "true" identity, states increasingly have granted adoptive adults access to their original birth certificates and adoption records. The "right to know," automatic in 1992 in only Alaska, Hawaii, and Kansas, has also fostered the practice of open adoption. This means adoptive parents allow natural parents visitation rights, or other limited, on-going communications about the child. It also makes it possible for the child to have communications with the birth parents later in life.

A family split resulted that was not resolved until the time of dad's death. Afterward, my aunt finally adopted my brother and changed his last name. In the meantime, strained relations limited communications within the family, especially between my brother and the rest of us siblings.

Consider what open adoption would mean if you applied this symbolically to your life. First, the parents who are losing their rights are the ones to whom you looked for love and support from childhood to maturity. We might call them our earth parents, transcending the distinction between birth, adoptive, foster parents, or other caregivers. The one who chooses to parent you would be you.

You choose to parent yourself. When you make this decision, parenting becomes an active process. You give up the legacy of the past, including being a slave to self-defeating habits. You assume the rights and responsibilities of a full member of humanity, including equal worth with your brothers and sisters. You develop a family-of-choice by adopting yourself first and then others as equal siblings. You legalize freedom of choice in your life. In the spirit of freedom and openness, you maintain on-going communications with your earth parents. This affirms the "and" in open adoption: communications are kept open between the parents of the past and the present parent, this being yourself.

Secondly, you may want to consider the benefits of investigating your parentage. If you have not looked back on your childhood and family-of-origin issues, then it could be helpful to identify both positive and negative aspects of your family inheritance. Many self-defeating habits that contribute to present unhappiness began in the past of childhood. To do this, you may need the assistance of an agency. In this case, psychotherapy or any other process of empowerment would be the agency of choice. Through the course of counseling, you would take several steps: investigate the effects of your childhood past; evaluate the suitability of your parentage; review specific incidents of hurt or neglect; and connect them with your present problems. This has become a popular activity in today's culture.

Finally, upon completion of the process of open adoption, there would be a new designation of parenthood. You assume the role. The difference between traditional parenting and this analogy is that you do the parenting within yourself. You parent other aspects of your personality. You develop a clear sense of a part of your personality that has all the positive traits of an adoptive parent. As these skills are developed, you learn to love yourself, including all the unlovable and undesirable parts. You also let these undesirable parts know who's in charge as you develop self-control.

This contributes to a new, expanded identity, as a worthwhile, mature, and responsible adult. You realize that who you are is the totality of the following: your name and who your parents were and your family and your greater family and a precious child of God. If you identify too closely with your parents, then you may let them become imitations of God. Also, you may mistakenly attribute negative aspects of your parents to God, thinking He is distant, or, unloving, or, punitive, or something else negative like your parents. The essence of your identity comes from God. How well you take care of yourself and what you make of your self is your responsibility as a mature adult. What you eventually make of yourself, you can give back to God as a gift. This expanded identity sets the stage for rebirth and higher-level parenting.

The many faces of parenting

Parenting is about many things. Basically, it involves providing love and structure that supports the child in his/her uniqueness. At its best, it includes the following categories: guiding, affirming, and nurturing. At its worst, parenting includes abuse and neglect. There are masculine and feminine versions of each category of parenting. Men parent differently from women. Also, men are more often guilty of neglecting their children than women. For some people, masculine parenting is synonymous with neglect. Neglect teaches self-neglect. Abuse perpetuates abuse. Since we relate best to feminine parenting styles, masculine methods of parenting are often misunderstood. For example, some mothers want fathers to be the disciplinarian. "I'm going to tell your daddy when he gets home," is the stereotypical maternal threat. Each style and category of parenting leaves an impression as the child matures, but may receive greater emphasis at various levels of child development.

Parenting Extremes

Look at parenting on a continuum. At the left extreme, you see abuse. Short of abuse, you can simply call it 'being strict.' On the right extreme, you see neglect. Short of neglect, you can call it 'indulgent.' Couples with opposite parenting styles experience conflict in the marital relationship and are often manipulated by the children. Parental abuse is related to self-abuse and other abuse. Parental neglect contributes to self-neglect and neglect of those people closest to you.

Effects of self-neglect

Some people practice emotional self-neglect because that is all they know. They were taught to not feel, not talk, and not trust. As the result, they internalized emotional self-neglect.

Consider how our unexpressed emotions influence our physical health. Stress jacks blood pressure. Fear and apprehension cause disruptions of the lower gastrointestinal tract. Repressed anger and bitterness may reduce resistance to infection, even some cancers. Negative emotions are generated by irrational, fear-based thoughts, beliefs, and attitudes. After time, one becomes paired with the other. When you feel depressed, negative thoughts appear or vice versa. One triggers the other.

Unexpressed emotions also affect our spiritual health. We approach spirituality with the intellect, questioning our faith excessively, sometimes to the point of reducing the notion of a Higher Power to material levels. Faith, like love, is incomplete without being experienced emotionally.

Denial is a unique form of self-neglect. It involves false beliefs and evasion of emotions, survival behaviors that were learned as a child. Denial also increases stress and promotes self-defeating behaviors. It allows problems to escalate to a crisis stage before responsible action is considered. This is practiced in dysfunctional families. When you deny your feelings, desires, and basic needs, problems intensify. When you act as though everything is fine when it is not, it is a "die" message for your body. Your body is like a child in many ways. It will do what it thinks your mind wants. This is how self-neglect helps perpetuate sickness.

Sickness is often practiced by parents instead of wellness. It can be expressed physically, emotionally, or spiritually. Parental behaviors usually speak louder than their words. One way or the other, a parent's negative messages get stuck in our heads. Here are some parental messages that promote sickness in a child and get carried into adult life:

- **"Don't pay attention to your body."** This gives adult children permission to eat plenty of junk food, drink too much, take drugs, and above all feel guilty about it. If you are over-stressed and tired, ignore it and keep pushing yourself.

- **"Life is meaningless and of little value."** This leaves an adult child with a "why bother" and "who cares" attitude.

- **"You have (should, ought) to do what I say."** This programs adult children to blindly respect age and authority. It teaches them to do the things they don't like and avoid doing what they really want. In this case, you might follow everyone else's opinions and advice, while seeing yourself as miserable and "stuck."

- **"Be resentful and hypercritical."** Critical and judgmental parents teach children the same skill. They become adults who judge, criticize, and nitpick, especially themselves.

- **"Fill your mind with dreadful pictures, then obsess over them."** Fear becomes the primary motivator. Adult children learn to worry most, if not all, of the time.

- "Avoid deep, lasting intimate relationships." This results in adults with intimacy difficulties, increases the negative effects of stress, and contributes to divorce.
- "Blame others for all your problems." This results in adult children who never get to solve their difficulties because they want to assign someone else the responsibility or blame.
- "Do not express your feelings and views openly and honestly." You are programmed to conform and believe that other people won't appreciate your open expression of feelings or views. You learn to prevent others from even knowing what your true thoughts and feelings are.
- "Shun anything that resembles a sense of humor." You come to believe that life is no laughing matter. You approach life with deadly seriousness and over-emphasize being practical.
- "Avoid making any changes." This contributes to an adult life-style that includes rigidity, resistance to change, and sticking with things even though they are killing somebody. Risks are avoided that would bring you greater satisfaction and joy.

Becoming more responsible involves self-care and overcoming self-neglect. You no longer delegate the responsibility to someone else or neglect yourself. Imagine that inside your personality remains a part of you that is the child you once were. This may be conceptualized as the totality of your childhood memories or simply as your inner child. This inner child can be thought of as embodying the essence of your personality, feelings, and soul. This is the part you can begin to parent as you focus on learning better skills in caring for yourself.

Now is the time to break out of self-denial, neglect, and abuse. I learned that, to the extent that I act like a responsible adult, then I'm free to act like a kid. Choose to adopt yourself and become your own parent. This means releasing the negative messages learned in childhood and making adult efforts to change self-defeating behaviors. At this very moment, the child within needs you to assume the role as a parent, as a mature, responsible adult. This gives you both freedom and responsibility. It promotes healing.

Effects of abuse

Abuse is usually remembered as a specific event, while neglect can be subtle and difficult to pinpoint. Extreme forms of abuse can be repressed for many years and re-surface later as a flashback. Whether remembered or repressed, abuse triggers defensive responses that can affect you the rest of your life.

Distrust, low self-esteem, learned helplessness, and secrecy are residual effects of abuse. False selves, such as people pleasers, are developed that protect a shamed little child who believes he is fundamentally flawed, lacking in worth and inherent goodness. These false selves and defensive behaviors dominate the personality of an abused person until he overcomes the mistaken belief that he lost something valuable, pure, and innocent to the abuser that he will never retrieve.

The truth is he just lost touch with this sense of value. An innocent little child waits in hiding until somebody begins acting as a mature, responsible adult. Only then will the child feel safe enough to find expression in your personality. This begins when you start parenting yourself better.

Resilience

Some children seem to be more immune from the negative effects of abuse and neglect. They seem to respond to the hurt of childhood with strength. Resilient children seem to make a successful adaptation despite being at risk from their dysfunctional and adverse family environments. Researchers have studied these children to learn how they differ from children who are more vulnerable. It seems these people are more than survivors because they have responded to adversity with healthy responses.

How do they differ? Their adaptation involves adoption. They adopt other people and ask for help when needed. They adopt healthy defenses and belief systems. They also seem to adopt themselves by finding a balanced form of self-reliance. I adapted somewhat. I found parent substitutes who watched over me and gave me advice and assistance. However, I was excessively self-reliant (at least in my mind). On the surface, resilient children seem to have adapted. A question comes to mind, "Have they adapted or are they just in denial?" It appears resilient children had adopted more than self-defeating survival skills. Consider this question and the habits of resilience while you explore better ways to parent yourself.

Positive parenting

There are many books available on parenting. Depending on the prevailing psychological influences, those books are slanted in different directions. Positive parenting can be found somewhere on the continuum between abuse and neglect, strictness and indulgent. Positive parenting also involves both parents finding one voice in their style and providing consistent, predictable parenting. It's also important that parents understand the developmental needs and age appropriate behaviors throughout a child's growing process. This takes adaptability. When parents omit necessary ingredients required for healthy adjustment and development all is not lost. You just get to fill it in yourself, usually after the fact in adulthood.

Nurturing your inner child

Parental nurturing means to help feed, protect, develop, and promote growth of the child. Small children need nurturing the most.

Masculine nurturing is sometimes difficult to recognize. This happens partially because of a prevailing assumption that fathers do not nurture. It is also confused because some women carry a lot of masculine energy which gets expressed in their mothering. Masculine methods are expressed by showing interest in the child, having fun, doing things the child is interested in, providing practical help, and being directive in a crisis-situation. A masculine approach to nurturing also might involve increasing talk with the child and expressing emotions through telling stories. When you adopt yourself, you can learn to nurture your inner child with both masculine and feminine styles.

Resilient children connect with other people who provide nurturing. They sense when situations are strange, untrustworthy, or not quite right. They distance from trouble during times of stress or disruption. They explore and experiment with their environment to combat feelings of helplessness. They use play and drama to compensate for loss and find comic relief in the tragic. They use judgment to separate good from bad and rely on their conscience to empower themselves with a sense of goodness.

Consider the following methods for tuning into your inner life and learning to nurture yourself:

-- buy a present for yourself, especially when you have reason to celebrate.

-- take yourself somewhere special (like on a vacation, retreat, favorite restaurant).

-- give yourself time to be alone & learn to relax in silence.

-- develop daily habits of prayer and meditation.

-- work on a personal growth program (like counseling, etc.) and make it a top priority.

-- keep a daily journal

-- permit others to love you

-- provide practical help to others and keep things in balance by saying "no" when you need to.

-- stay in good physical shape by exercising and watching your diet.

-- have fun and play with your friends

-- express positive and negative emotions and tell other people stories of your life

-- know how to take and record vital signs from your body

-- perform basic first aid procedures

-- keep a properly stocked medicine cabinet

-- perform regular breast or testicular self-examinations

-- get a flu shot in the fall

-- use sun screen in the summer

-- be decisive and directive in a crisis

-- can you list others?

Maintain an awareness of your habits or routine behaviors. If they seem neglectful or self-abusive, then you can make changes. This begins with learning how to nurture yourself. Next, practice daily. Correct practice is the key for healthy habit formation.

Guiding the inner adolescent

Guiding involves showing a child the way, directing him, and leading him. An older child or adolescent requires lots of guidance. Masculine styles of guiding are often negative, heavy-handed, intrusive, and laden with excessive advice or punishment. A more positive approach to masculine guidance involves giving equal amounts of listening coupled with advice. It involves showing interest in the teenager's activities and providing leadership. Since adolescents tend toward distortion of viewpoints, masculine guidance also can involve monitoring irrational thoughts, considering options, and teaching compromise. There is a part of us that is still like a teenager emotionally. We are emotionally immature, rebellious, and self-centered. This part calls for guidance and attention from your parental self.

A resilient adolescent recruits other people as surrogate parents when guidance is desired. They know when a situation has become a problem and will disengage or distance physically when trouble disrupts. They work toward goals and explore a wide range of interests. As an artist, they shape and transform the pain and ugliness of life into metaphors, images, and symbols. Resilient teenagers see their parents' troubled behaviors as absurd. In spite of a negative example, they develop values based on principles.

In the following space are some methods for tuning into your inner adolescent and learning to guide yourself:

    -- ask your inner teenager what he/she wants when facing decisions.

    -- admit that you need others and honor your decision to ask for help.

    -- listen to yourself and know how you are coming across to others.

    -- learn to negotiate and compromise.

    -- develop and show an interest in your life, work, friends, and yourself.

    -- learn your leadership style and share your personal power.

    -- know who to call in an emergency, including professionals.

    -- take proper care of your body: nutrition, exercise, rest, play, and self-respect.

    -- keep medical history records (including allergies to medications)

    -- keep dental history records (including regular performance of dental hygiene--brushing, flossing, plaque identification)

    -- can you list others?

Use this list to test your current level of guidance habits. If you are not satisfied, then do something differently. If you keep doing the same things, then you can only expect more of the same. All behaviors are acted out at least twice. First, they are rehearsed in the mind with thoughts, beliefs, and attitudes. Later, they are acted out in your physical behaviors. Change involves informing yourself of a new, better way to live, paying conscious attention to the desired behaviors, and practicing regularly.

Affirming your adult self

Affirming involves giving support, encouragement, and approval. Affirmations are important along the developmental cycle, but are often most wanted by young adult children. To make a healthy break from home, a young adult needs two things: affirmations, like "you're gonna be OK" and parental blessings. These are often available from feminine voices, but lacking from masculine voices. Parental disapproval is communicated both verbally and non-verbally. What is not said can sometimes be as damaging as hurtful words. Blessings and other communications of love are often withheld or available only with strings attached.

Resilient adults develop an understanding and mature regard for theirs and others' well-being. They surround themselves with others who affirm and support their goals. They have a tolerance for complexity and ambiguity while generating pleasure in completing difficult projects. They express emotions through artistic outlets and laugh at their emotional pain. They respond to their difficulties with an obligation to serve others, society, and the world.

At the end of the developmental cycle, adult children often find themselves parenting their elderly parents. At this stage, nurturing and guidance become important and are most accepted by an aging parent if offered with affirmations. This can be very difficult if an adult child has unresolved conflicts with their elderly parents. In either case, your adoptive parent serves as an immediate source of affirmations for adult aspects of your personality.

Inadequate masculine parenting skills result in negative consequences. For example, lack of masculine approval contributes to performance-based self worth. Absentee or distant fathers leave children to form images of masculinity that have little factual basis. Since many children have not received adequate masculine parenting, they often do not develop realistic masculine parenting skills themselves. These skills are often lacking or undeveloped in men and women.

Use the following ideas to tune into your inner self and learn to affirm yourself:

-- talk to yourself with a comforting voice.

-- associate with people who affirm you, honor your self-love and share enthusiasm for your goals in life.

-- get to know yourself by journaling your family history, your personality traits, your dreams, flashes of insight, major victories, and so forth.

-- say to yourself, "I'm gonna be OK."

-- manage your life resources: money, time, affection, energy, and so forth.

-- seek the blessings of significant others when you make major changes

-- listen to your conscience and be honest with yourself and others.

-- stand up for yourself when you need to.

-- imitate no one, unless it's your Higher Power.

-- develop your imagination and creativity.

-- take responsibility for things you do and say as well as what you fail to do.

-- forgive yourself and others

-- realize that God loves you, imperfections and all.

-- can you list others?

Audio tapes and daily meditation calendars are often helpful reminders of the importance of becoming skillful in affirming yourself. External aides can be helpful while you are developing an internal voice of affirmation.

By choosing open adoption, you cease your search for someone to adopt you. You adopt yourself. You no longer settle for temporary foster care. You no longer look for parenting in your adult relationships or parent other adults in relationships. You avoid self-neglect and self-abuse. You become your own adoptive parent, incorporating the best of masculine and feminine skills. You learn positive ways to take care of yourself, becoming more self-reliant and interdependent.

Self-parenting

The problem with parenting yourself as an adult is that you are playing catch up for your various needs and developmental requirements that were absent. You may be developmentally stuck in some areas. Therefore, you focus will change from time to time depending on how you assess your problem. Knowing the parts of your personality and their psychological age will help. Every part to your personality, like a player in an orchestra, has specific traits and maturities. Like the oboe player, there are identifiable thoughts, beliefs and attitudes that are specific to the oboe player. There are identifiable emotions and physical actions uniquely related to that instrumentalist. They can be associated with that particular part of the personality and an estimate of the psychological age estimated. From this base, you can begin to parent yourself more deliberately.

Self-care

Self-care is an approach to health care that makes the client or patient, rather than the therapist or doctor, the primary health resource. Self-care is the self-initiated and self-controlled application of knowledge necessary for the promotion of health. It involves reduction of undesired risk, self-diagnosis and treatment of some problems, and, where appropriate, effective and self-protected uses of professional mental and physical health care resources. Self-care can be thought of as comprising three categories: health maintenance, wellness-oriented behaviors, and care of self during illness.

It would be better if the goals of therapists were to foster development of 'activated' clients. These are clients who accept more responsibility for their own health. They learn skills of observing common self-defeating behaviors and managing common problems. They increase their understanding of the effect of corrective behaviors on well-being and become knowledgeable of the health care process. Thus, they become better medical consumers. They make the most efficient use of therapeutic services.

Sadly, I had to learn much of this on my own and in my adult years. In my opinion, too many therapists are enablers who hold their clients' hands and reinforce their self-defeating beliefs. Therapists pick up where the parents leave off: being neglectful, enablers, and/or too indulgent.

The goals of your self-care efforts may be two-fold:

(1) to evaluate and improve your health without waiting for unwanted symptoms to occur, and

(2) to help you cope with illness, both through self-care and by making effective use of health care support when needed.

Therefore, self-care helps prevent unwanted problems. It also enhances coping and recovery when problems do occur. Finally, self-care contributes to happiness and promotes more enjoyable relationships.

Self-care behaviors have been shown to play a significant role in management of many chronic problems, such as alcohol and other drug addictions, depression, ADHD, stress, hypertension, arthritis, diabetes, and cancer, in some cases. For example, studies have shown that clients with alcoholism who take an active role in their own recovery are more likely to be in control of their problems. They may have a chronic illness, but do not suffer from unwanted symptoms as much when they take an active role and do what they know works.

Structured self-care programs, such as the 12-step programs, view the client as a decision-maker and problem-solver. The client is ultimately in charge of the problem, but accepts the help and support of the group. The professional serves as an advisor and guide. Instead of denial, the client uses his radar to recognize emerging problems. He believes that it is okay to have problems. With detachment, he maintains a healthy perspective. Believing it's okay to ask for help, he is willing to act and include others in his self-care efforts, when needed.

Self-help

Self-care works best when working jointly with people dedicated to helping each other. Self-help support groups, such as Alcoholics Anonymous, are popular in the United States. It has been estimated that there are over one-half million self-help groups with a total membership of more than 15 million persons. The moral inventories and spiritual aspects of 12-step support groups provide a useful program for internalizing values through actual discovery of spiritual principles. This is important in parenting because it helps instill the value of self-care and leads to the maintenance of health and development of wellness-oriented behaviors.

Although experimental research with self-help groups is limited and lacks sophistication, the research that does exist shows positive results. Self-help groups enjoy wide popularity because they are economical. They also are widely accredited with helping people avoid excessive and dysfunctional behaviors through supportive relationships that nurture the recovery process.

Self-help materials, such as brochures, booklets, CD/DVD's, books (preferably workbooks), and educational seminars enjoy increasing acceptance by professionals and consumers. They provide concrete products to people, are generally regarded as helpful, and facilitate delivery of services to as many people as possible. Even movies can be used independently or as an adjunct to counseling.

A self-help manual is as effective as ten sessions of self-control training provided by an experienced therapist, according to research by psychologists in New Mexico. Self-help materials that are based on principles of self-management theory can assist people in avoiding problematic behaviors. These principles work best with chronic problems when applied as a part of therapy. Alternative applications may include using self-help techniques with only minimal contact with a counselor. Self-help methods may be viewed as a prelude to psychotherapy, adjunct to care during treatment, and principal tool in maintenance and continuing care following therapy. Therefore, self-help methods can be viewed as the alpha and omega of learning to take better care of yourself.

Hearing the signals

Emotional and physical upset can be viewed as a warning message from our bodies. These upsets tell us that somewhere we are not following our true energy or honoring our feelings and desires. The body gives us many such signals, beginning with subtle feelings of dissatisfaction, tiredness, restlessness, discomfort, irritation, anxiety, or sadness.

If we don't listen to these cues and take corrective action, our bodies will give us stronger signals. These usually come as aches (including heartaches), frustration, anger, pains, and minor illnesses.

If we still don't heed the warnings, a serious illness or accident may eventually occur. Minor depression becomes major. Anxiety attacks occur and send us to the emergency room thinking we are having a heart attack. We lose control of our anger and experience attacks of rage. The stronger messages can usually be avoided by paying attention to the subtler ones. Once a strong message has come, it is never too late to be healed, if that is what you truly desire.

Turning up the volume

To improve your health, you must become an expert on your thoughts, feelings, needs, and desires. You begin by tuning into yourself, especially your thought processes. Emotions can teach you what you desire and what you are thinking. They are loyal to your thoughts, like dogs are to humans. Tuning into yourself means learning how to monitor your self-talk and self-defeating habits.

Self-care is an attitude toward yourself and your life that says, "I am responsible for myself. I am responsible for living or not living my life. I am responsible for tending to my emotional, physical, spiritual, and financial well-being. I am responsible for identifying and meeting my needs and desires. I am responsible for solving my problems and for my own choices. I am responsible for what I give and receive and for setting and achieving my goals." It is an attitude of freedom of choice and respect for yourself. Therefore, make life-giving choices and avoid the ones that stifle life.

Attitudes change and develop through three different pathways: compliance, identification, and internalization. Movement from the first toward the last represents maturity, growth, and development.

Compliance. In this path, a person or group accepts influence from another person or group because they hope to achieve favorable reactions from the other, such as getting approval or rewards, or to avoid punishment.

Compliance is what happens when laws are created, or rules are laid down by a person or small group in authority. Its success depends on the "carrot" of rewards or the "stick" of fear of punishment. If a group requires heavy amounts of compliance, its members will have less control over their lives. Beneath their compliance may lie a repressed hatred.

Identification. In this path, an individual adopts the behavior of another person or group in order to join. This establishes mutually supportive relationships. Change in this case comes not from coercion or promised reward, but because the person wants affiliation.

Identification involves membership and is part of group formation, as well as human development. It is heavily dependent on external conditions rather than internal needs and desires. If a group works this way, it makes people very malleable and insecure, for it supports fads and charismatic people of all persuasions who easily move others to follow their whims.

Dysfunctional groups such as cults and gangs use both compliance and identification selectively to program their members. It is no wonder why their members often feel helpless and insecure. To break away from these unhealthy patterns, you must learn to think for yourself and learn how to evaluate information, critically. This leads you to the next pathway.

Internalization. In this path, there is a behavioral and attitude change that arises from within a person or group, as the result of careful consideration of things and of judging "What's good for me?"

When people's actions spring from a clear motive of doing what is in their best interests, they are acting from a sense of internalization. For internalization to occur we must be able to access and appreciate the roots of the experience of being human and to keep our roots alive and renewed. We also must know the steps of discernment or spiritual decision-making.

Ask yourself these questions: "Which path did you follow in forming attitudes toward yourself?" Did you come by your attitudes naturally or have you adopted them after careful consideration?

The masculine or active method of getting our needs met, using a positive approach, is to go for it. At times, we need to move toward a certain goal daringly. To fail to do so may mean we resort to a more negative approach, such as manipulation or attempting to control people.

At other times, we need to practice the feminine or receptive method, which, when used positively, is to attract the object of your desires to you. This involves practicing nurturing ourselves, appreciating ourselves, and becoming attuned to our inner selves so that we can attract and receive what we want. To fail to do so may mean we regress to a more negative approach involving moodiness and pouting when we don't get what we want.

Many people are developed on only one side. Some people know how to go after things, but have a tough time attracting things to them. Others know how to attract things but are afraid to go after them directly. Often a balancing process is necessary. You may want to stretch your ability to receive the gifts of appreciation and love coming to you. Conversely, you may want to consider the benefits of directly asking for what you want and observing the results. Look for areas that you can develop and get to work. It contributes to balance.

Many people use things such as sex, food, drugs and alcohol, relationships, or other compulsive behaviors as substitutes for parenting. They attempt to feed themselves emotionally and spiritually through material means. These are self-defeating methods. The key to learning to parent yourself is to trust your feelings and intuition, monitor your thoughts, and take responsible action. To do this, you must make a conscious effort to tune into what you want, make sure it's healthy to want it, and take some risks.

Parenting yourself in relationships

How do you attract people to you? Some people play the role of a child and attract parental figures as friends and partners. Others play the role of victim. This role mostly attracts people who rescue or victimize. Sometimes a partner plays out both roles, initially rescuing and later abusing you. Consider the relative health of your method of attracting people.

One important way to attract a romantic partner is to be healthy. Health, vitality, a sense of fun and enthusiasm make so many young people appealing even when they aren't particularly handsome or beautiful. Health and vigor are even more appealing in the middle and older years, partly because a well-kept body is rare in these age groups. People do let themselves go. And other people aren't apt to love and admire them if they obviously don't love and admire themselves. Answer these questions: "How do you attract attention to yourself?" Does your state of health reflect how you treat yourself? Let your answers guide you to corrective action.

The most important key to creating and maintaining good health is learning to assert yourself consistently in your life. Some people with health problems usually have a pattern of doubting themselves, of being afraid to trust their feelings and act on them. They especially need to learn how to say "no" to others when they don't want to do something. "No" can be a complete sentence when used assertively.

Other people with health problems don't have strong personal boundaries. They try to please and take care of others. In the process, they allow others to intrude on them and take advantage of them. Thus, they resort to using ill health as a buffer, a way of creating some distance from people.

Ask yourself, "What is my body trying to tell me?" Are you listening? Is anybody listening to the child inside who needs something?

This inter-linkage between all our personality parts is important in building relationships. Self-knowledge, self-forgiveness, and awareness contribute to a solid foundation of emotional integrity. This increases honesty with ourselves and others. Upon that we can make such powerful statements as "I forgive you" or "I love you" that echo to the very core. From a whole person comes complete forgiveness and a solid love.

We first learn about relationships from observing our parents. This is called a "partnering" relationship in a family, referring to the quality of the relationship between mother and father. Consider how your parents "partnered" each other. In other words, evaluate the nature, strength, and quality of their relationship. This gives insights regarding how you learned to behave or how not to behave in primary relationships. Partnering is an executive function in a family that involves being lovers, best friends, playmates, financial decision-makers, and planners. In many families, these were not positive models. Therefore, we need new, healthy models of both parenting and partnering to move forward in our quest for health and happiness in relationships.

These new models are often learned with the assistance of a counselor, who may function as a foster parent because of the temporary nature of the relationship. It is through the work with a counselor that you learn new skills of parenting yourself. Books and other self-help resources serve a similar purpose.

To the extent that you learn to parent yourself, you can parent others better. Remember the best gift you can give your inner child, or any other child is a healthy, well-adjusted parent.

Parenting yourself & raising children

You would be well-advised to avoid taking responsibility for more children than you can parent. In my case, there were too many children for the number of parents. My father was probably overwhelmed and was unable to give enough love and attention. This was one of several sources of stress for a single father who never intended to have to raise the children alone. When the source of love became scarce, my brothers and sisters began to compete for daddy's time and attention. Sibling rivalry developed. Some children felt lost and ignored. Others enjoyed a special status with their father, although it was not necessarily a positive benefit in the long run. As children, they became either experienced at competing for someone else's love and attention, or they resigned themselves to settle for what little they could get. This carried over into their adult relationships.

This is why adoptive parenting is so important. It puts the focus where it belongs, on yourself. When you adopt yourself, you do not have to compete for the limited care of another person or take responsibility for parenting a romantic partner. It also frees you be a healthier parent for your children.

Children best learn about the world from adults, not from other children. In many places, children are running in gangs, being taught by other children. In other places adults are seeking quick fixes, answers, and affiliation in seminars and retreats only to find themselves entangled in cult-like groups. In dysfunctional environments, the primary lessons are about survival no matter how they are camouflaged. Children need adults modeling healthy behaviors in order to learn about health and happiness. Adults are responsible for their own discernment.

Each child brought into the world requires at least one adult committed to and able to focus full attention. If the parent is unavailable, there must be adequate resources to secure alternate childcare. Many birth mothers give their child up for adoption because they have little finances or family support to assist in childcare. It is a value judgment. A parent has a right to decline caring for the child alone. We all can benefit from having down time to pursue career and leisure goals. Only the most overprotective parent would totally subordinate themselves to the needs of a child. Therefore, the decision to provide alternate childcare or to give a child up for adoption can be a great act of love and concern for the child's best interests.

Does this suggest that adults who both work should avoid having any children? This is not necessarily true. Eventually, humans will learn to extend their families beyond blood ties - adopt each other informally. In this way, someone else will be able to provide one-on-one attention to children. All the love does not have to come from the parents alone. It is better if it does not. This is another value judgment. In ancient Rome and Sparta childcare was provided by non-parents, usually for military and political reasons. However, the child needs one-on-one love and attention from the caregiver in addition to training and education. When we learn to adopt each other, childcare will be provided by non-parents for spiritual reasons.

In this regard, we must always strive to find a way to know and speak the truth with love. It is important to tell a child the truth. This provides someone present in the child's life, who gives love and attention, answers his questions truthfully, and protects him. This makes it easier for a child to grasp greater truths about God's love and protection.

Spiritual parenting

As we grasp the notion of adoptive parenting, it sets the stage for higher parenting. We can develop a greater sense of family with God as the father, earth as mother of the Holy Spirit, and Christ as a brother who shares the human experience. This means that adults must strive for a way of relating to all people, adults and children, by focusing on them in a way that sends them love. This way of consciously relating, in which everyone attempts to bring out the best in others, is a posture the entire human race must eventually adopt to survive.

Adoptionism is a controversial theological doctrine that was propounded in the 8th century by a Spanish bishop who attempted to distinguish between the divine and human natures of Christ. He argued that, in his divinity, Christ was the son of God by nature. However, in his humanity, Christ was the son of God by adoption only. It is assumed that the argument is based on the idea that Jesus was not conceived by Joseph. Jesus had no biological father. God was his Creator. This raises the following question: Was Christ adopted by Joseph? The Son of God, a precious child of God, adopted by earthly parents. The scripture is not clear, and this argument will be left for others to consider. If Christ was adopted, what is the message for us?

In the Holy Bible, at least one author uses adoption to show the strength of God's relationship with us. To summarize, the scripture says God has adopted us as his children. He chose us. Abba is the Aramaic word for father. It was used by Christ in his prayers. As adopted children of God, we share with Jesus all rights to God's resources. Through Jesus' sacrifice, God has brought us into his family and made us heirs along with Jesus. As God's heirs, we can claim what he has provided for us, our full identity as his children.

We are all chosen by God, by the ones who love us, by adoptive ones. Therefore, adoptive ones are the ones who choose to love us. By choosing to love

God first and ourselves as each other, we become God's chosen people. Likewise, when a person chooses a spiritual path, he or she claims all the privileges and responsibilities of a child in God's family. He claims the goodness of his nature and identifies himself as a precious child of God.

One of these outstanding privileges is being led by the spirit. This involves responsible consciousness, maintaining awareness. Conscious relating brings conscious growth and evolution. It also involves surrender. This leads to a significantly different way of life that bears fruit. We know we are being led by the spirit when we have peace. It also helps to consult the Holy Scriptures and follow our conscience. Remember to ask for wisdom when making decisions about following the spirit.

Many years have passed since I became an orphan. I consciously attached myself to parent substitutes to fill the void left when my parents died. Many were chosen: teachers, sisters, brothers, employers, in-laws, and others who temporarily served a parental function. Later, I learned to parent myself. Gradually, I realized that earth parents are only temporary by spiritual design. Now, I acknowledge the Creator of the universe as my true Father who conceived all creatures. Earth is my mother. By practicing adoptive parenting, I have become a co-creator with God. I claim my rightful place as an equal heir of this good earth.

If you seek the spirit, it can be found. Practice working in peace. Call the Kingdom of Heaven from the unseen world into the present moment of everyday existence. Practice surrender. Spirit will come.

When we adopt each other and give love unconditionally, we receive love in return because of the way love interacts in the universe. Our personal love is not enough. Unconditional love comes from God or from people with a close walk with God in their lives. As we connect to God, we tap into the source of unconditional love that must be given away. When we give unconditional love, it comes from an overflow. We are both fulfilled and overflowing with love. This creates currents in the flow of love that increase in intensity as love flows through us to others. It starts a chain reaction, much like the butterfly effect, in which a butterfly's wings fluttering in China creates a thunderstorm in New York. It begins a process that literally sends love around the world and back again. Begin this process today by adopting yourself!

Notes

CHAPTER 4

MIRRORS: VIEWING LIFE'S EXPERIENCES AS A TEACHER

Once, while visiting a drug rehabilitation center, I noticed a mirror with a sign over it saying:

Look in the mirror to see who is really responsible for your problems.

"Why was this mirror there?" I asked myself. Perhaps it was to stimulate my curiosity and teach me lessons, like that of the clients there.

My interest in mirrors stems from this single experience. It was perpetuated by a 30-year period of studying, helping, and being helped. This interest grew through the process of reading books, viewing videos, listening to recordings, and writing, counseling clients, and receiving some very good guidance myself. It was this curiosity I followed that led to collecting and integrating material on the symbolism of mirrors. The outcome was to increase my awareness in viewing life's experiences as a teacher.

I learned that mirrors are important therapeutic tools, both literally and symbolically. Looking at oneself can be a humbling process. Humility, self-examination, and recovery go together. To overcome denial, we must take a long, hard look at ourselves. So, when people stop long enough from drinking, working, worrying, or any of the other activities of life that dominate our time to look closely in a mirror, they can begin to see reflections everywhere that can be instructive.

Our thoughts, emotions, and behaviors give us an ongoing reflection of ourselves and our desires. However, we must take the time and effort to look closely. The world is like a giant mirror that reflects both our spirits and our forms. Once we have learned how to look into this mirror, see clearly, and interpret its reflection, we have a potent tool for personal growth.

I also learned the technical aspects of therapeutic mirrors. Mirroring is a term originated by S.H. Foulkes and comes from group therapy literature. It is a natural process. In group therapy, it is considered a potent contributor to therapeutic gain. The intent of mirroring is to restore the ego state and confirm its integrity through the constant practice of honest communication. Mirror reactions are brought about when a person sees himself, often a disowned part of the self, reflected in the interactions of another person in a therapy group. In his research, Foulkes noted that a person in a group sees another group member reacting in the way he/she does himself, or, sometimes, in contrast to his own behavior. In this manner, we get to know hidden aspects of ourselves. This is a fundamental process in ego development that usually begins in the group structure of a family. As we grow and develop in childhood, we learn about ourselves by the effect we have on others and the image they form of us. Thus, mirror reactions refer both to the developmental process and the therapeutic process. It reflects who we have been, who we are, and who we will become.

In therapy groups, the mirroring phenomenon is sometimes structured through the assignment of a specific group member as a mirror imager. The Mirror Imager (MI) is someone who has already successfully completed an earlier treatment phase and is assigned to the group as a participant-observer and resource. Paradoxically, its major purpose is for further treatment gains of the MI as opposed to being a primary benefit to the group. A person's denial is often reinforced by psychological isolation and distance. Mirror imaging weakens the denial by placing the MI in the group structure where he or she is subject to the thought processes and experiences of others. In this context, the MI hears many conceivable forms of denial and is reminded of his universal ploys to hide from reality. The group members receive secondary benefits by witnessing the MI struggling with some of the basic ongoing issues of life. They are reminded that there are no quick fixes. This experience also gives other group members a chance to see issues they may anticipate struggling with in the future. This structured approach to mirror imaging seems to be an unusual and powerful tool. Everyone involved benefits.

So, I learned several useful concepts in establishing mirroring as a metaphor. Literally, a mirror is a piece of reflecting glass that enables a person to see his own image. It reflects light and shows images. Other surfaces also act as mirrors, such as water in a lake. Reflections are the images formed and revelations received from reflected light. Mirror reactions are simply the rapid action of light being reflected from the surface of a mirror to the person. Mirror images are what is seen by looking closely in the mirror. In Latin, the word for mirror is <u>speculum</u>. A root word of speculation, it is defined as an image or as reflection <u>and</u> contemplation.

Metaphorically, mirroring is about psychological reflection, contemplation, and learning from life's experiences. In this sense, people, animals, and experiences are mirrors (or mirror imagers) who reflect lessons about life and the art of living. Like any learning process, it takes time to obtain answers. Learning time is involved in any process. Applied symbolically, mirroring involves dedicating time for practice, reflection, and contemplation. Places of reflection can be anywhere that is conducive to contemplation. Mirror reactions are about seeing ourselves in others and consciously using this information to expand our sense of who we are. This involves looking inward and stretching our self-identity. It also involves practice, which is about trial and error. Practice takes time, too. Some people are easily frustrated because they want quick answers or mistakenly believe that they should be able to do it right the first time. Mirror imagers can be people we have given formal permission to act as mirrors, such as a counselor, sponsor, guide, mentor, or teacher. In the process of working with these mirror imagers, we can trust that they will probably also benefit. Informal mirror imagers can be anyone or any experience from which we learn and apply the positive lessons of life.

In this sense, the mirror became a metaphor that helped me see the world as a teacher. I learned to view life experiences as a mirror to teach me hidden aspects about myself that I couldn't see directly. This metaphor stands on two assumptions:

1) I assumed that everything in my life is my reflection, my partial creation; all accidents or events relate to me. There are no simple coincidences. If I saw or felt something and if it had any impact on me, then a part of me had attracted or created it to show me something. If it didn't mirror some part of myself, then I couldn't even see it. Therefore, all the experiences, animals, and people in my life reflect various characters and feelings that represent parts of my personality.

2) I learned to avoid putting myself down for the reflections I saw. I knew that nothing was entirely negative. Every experience is a gift that brings me to self-awareness and increased understanding. I am here to learn and, in some cases, re-learn. I am an imperfect human being, like every person. I maintained a compassionate attitude toward myself and my learning process (most of the time!). This involved asking for help, seeking teachers, and granting myself time to learn. To the extent that I could do these things, the learning process, which is life itself, became fun and interesting.

To apply this metaphor to yourself ask these three questions:

1) How can I use my experiences in the world as a mirror?

2) How can I act as a mirror with my friends and loved ones?

3) How does the past mirror my present experiences?

Past lessons: Who we have been

As we know, mirrors literally play a significant role in a person's identity formation during adolescence. It is normal for adolescents to be extremely preoccupied with how they look. As a teenager, I spent endless hours looking in the mirror, not only at my clothes, but at my face, my developing body, and other features, good or bad. As I looked in the mirror I was in a very tangible way trying to figure out who I was, seeking to discern in those reflections, an identity. Little did I know how many years it would take me to complete this process.

Childhood mirrors

There's a lot of pride and self-centeredness in this behavior. That same pride or self-preoccupation before mirrors is quick to be wounded. Adolescents do not take kindly to criticism, especially when unsolicited. While pride is a healthy and necessary part of the process of identity formation, a vicious, self-defeating pride can develop. When this happens, it creates a sensitivity to criticism. A resistance to change often results which is reflected in a "love me or leave me alone," or "like it or lump it" attitude. To get past this stage, we must learn to overcome pride and selfishness.

In childhood, adolescence, and early adulthood, people often form dependent relationships. During this time, patterns can develop which repeat themselves throughout the life cycle. These relationships are like a mirror, except with a different focus. We see ourselves reflected in someone or something else. Our worth, our ambitions, our security, our hopes and dreams are all projected onto careers or significant other people, such as spouses, best friends, or even in group membership. Sooner or later this causes problems in relationships because of self-neglect. This long term self-neglect usually brings on depression or other emotional problems. Little do we realize that behind the mirror that we look into, hoping to see what we want to see, is a separate person. We might be better able to love this person if we let go of control, preconceived notions, and self-defeating attitudes and beliefs.

Parental mirrors

Parents often are confused about their reflected needs and the needs of their children. Finding happiness requires that we learn to tell the difference between our needs and the reflected needs of someone else. For example, parents reinforce compulsive behavior in their children by stressing excellence in sports, academic, or social worlds. This results in a performance-based sense of worth. When children fail, parents react anxiously, viewing it as a negative reflection on themselves. In other ways, parents often attempt to re-live their lives through their children by giving them things they wanted for themselves at that age, often without noticing how it's hurting the children. Therefore, parents frequently either take too much pride in their children's accomplishments, or leave them feeling they were never good or grateful enough. Either way damages a child's self-concept.

Mirror images

Be careful in applying this metaphor to past experiences. We often make mistakes and learn only negative lessons from past experiences. In tense, harsh or painful childhood experiences, it's easy to get a negative lesson from a mirroring experience.

As a little boy, I once became angry when a barnyard rooster attacked my younger brother. My father whipped me with a board for shouting a curse-word. Unable to help my brother and frozen in fear, I unconsciously began to fear my anger and became enslaved to saving others. I was distracted and shamed by the beating. That little boy went into hiding. Before the boy would come back out of hiding, I had to learn the positive lessons in this experience. These lessons directed me to develop a mature self that can stand up to abuse without counterattacking, while keeping a focus on what is wanted (not unwanted), and believing that goodness will prevail in the circumstances of life.

Mirror images also reverse themselves. For example, after my mother died, I unconsciously developed a pattern of expecting pain, death, or failure in the face of joy, birth, or success. I moved forward in life unintentionally sabotaging my best efforts. To correct this self-defeating pattern, I had to face that part of me that was like Wylie Coyote, the cartoon character. I had to quit causing things to backfire on me. Since reflections can be misinterpreted by making negative transfers or reversing images, caution is necessary. Professional assistance is sometimes required to avoid becoming stuck in self-defeating behavior patterns.

In addition, we need to learn to be aware of how we absorb, which is the opposite of reflection. For example, companion animals, such as dogs, will absorb released raw emotional energy. When released during an argument, dogs will act on it by coming to the people involved and insisting on kind and caring attention. This is something the people arguing needed to do for themselves. Other times, a dog will respond to what it's absorbing by simply reflecting its owners' emotions in its own behavior, such as withdrawing inside itself, showing hurt and distrust, or even attacking others viciously. Adolescents often do this with parents by taking on their parents' guilt and shame or acting out the dysfunction in their marriage. Remember, your family is a mirror, too. It reflects the nature of the world, which runs on both virtue and evil.

Present lessons: Who we are

You may sometimes wonder why you make mistakes when you truly want to do better. It is a natural part of the human experience. Mistakes are often needed to teach you a lesson. Some lessons cannot be learned without difficulty. So learn your lessons, quickly, by overcoming the obstacles in life. The overcoming is not about the one who troubled you, but the overcoming of the darkness in your own nature.

Self-mirrors

How do you overcome mistaken beliefs about yourself and quit repetitive patterns of self-neglect? The past and the future are simply reflections of an everlasting now. In this ongoing present reality, we connect to those memories and experiences with people who came before and to those who will come after. It is important to realize that while people come and go in your life, you are always there. Continuity is found within. Therefore, it helps to find a way to be comfortable knowing who you are, what you desire, and how to ask for it. This involves learning to love yourself unconditionally, including the undesirable and unlovable parts of your personality.

While this sounds simple, a major commitment to personal growth is often required to find these answers. Working a personal growth program requires ability in taking action and in concurrently reflecting on this action to learn from it. Personal growth requires discipline in both action and reflection by using a scientific approach to problem-solving. Therefore, it is helpful to use problem-solving methods and take action. Remember to set aside quiet time to calm yourself, reflect on the results, and center on love. This combination of reflection and action amounts to the art and science of personal growth.

A person's ego is by nature a reflection. It can be either a good, sharp, clear image or it can simply be a fuzzy illusion, such as seeing yourself as independent. Paradoxically, people with a fuzzy sense of self often attach themselves to a powerful person, like a mentor, by mirroring their attitudes and tastes. If a person believes in these illusions, then he will go to a great deal of trouble to keep up appearances. These people spend a lot of time and energy promoting their image, both professionally and personally. In contrast, a person who sees himself as interdependent will openly admit that he needs others. His ego becomes a working partner with his Higher Power, spouse, and life itself. He makes a good partner, who cooperates and co-creates with God.

Nature's mirrors

Mirrors help you see your true image more clearly. They appear through people, in experiences, and, even in animals. For example, I observed the dog and how it absorbs negative emotions from its owner. I noticed how the coyote mirrored my acts of self-sabotage. Next, I considered the wolf, my namesake and an animal that has a controversial image. I could easily recognize the dark side of the wolf due to years of popular programming in modern society. I did not necessarily want to look at my dark nature. However, there were very gentle aspects of the wolf that, for a long time, I had overlooked, but came to own within myself. Look closely into the psyche of the wolf and you will see a reflection of yourself.

Wolves are predators. They may prey upon animals larger than them, but single out the weak: very old or very young, sick and lame. They prey by stalking them, sneaking up on them, ambushing them, or ganging up on them until they give in. The phrase "a wolf at the door" has been used for ages as a metaphor for looming bad times that leave the unprepared feeling victimized.

Wolves are victims. As a species, they have been singled out for elimination and discrimination. The wolf has become a symbol for something negative that isn't understood or controlled, a thing to be avoided or disowned. Wolves have been victimized for years by the government, by Hollywood, and in myths or fairy tales with labels like "big bad wolf" and "werewolf."

Wolves are rescuers. According to Native American legend, the wolf is our teacher, also called a way-shower. Native people learned much about survival from the wolves. For example, survival strategies such as stealth, ambush, and careful use of resources were learned from observing the wolves. In this manner, wolves may have indirectly rescued primitive humans from starvation. To return the favor of being rescued, humans turned on the wolves. Eventually, wolves learned to keep their distance.

Compare yourself to the wolf by asking the following questions. Have you ever helped someone or tried to care for someone who eventually turned on you? How do you play the victim role? Are you aware of the predator within you? In what ways do you persecute or victimize yourself? If you feel victimized, look around for your persecutor. Also, realize that you may be in need of a rescuer or savior. How do you rescue? Has it occurred to you that you can rescue yourself? These three roles are often learned in childhood, then played in both your inner life and outer world in a triangular-shaped pattern.

Humans and wolves are alike in other ways. Both humans and wolves use rituals that reinforce relationships, maintain order, and enforce discipline. Both are territorial. Human tribes and wolf packs both consist largely of family-like units. Both rely on rules of behavior that govern society. And both select, in their own ways, leaders possessing the necessary abilities to get things done.

Wolves and humans are both defensive. Wolves mirror our defensiveness. Foulkes conceded that mirroring can be discussed in terms of defense mechanisms, such as identification, projection, and so forth, suggesting we consider these phenomena collectively as elements of the mirror effect. Consider the idea that primitive humans learned some useful defensive traits from wolves. Some examples of these useful survivor skills are suggested below.

Wolves are observers. They take in essential information visually. Wolves are intimate with the world around them. They are careful observers. They live in the present moment. They watch, and they learn. They teach the importance of being watchful of behaviors to see if people "walk like they talk."

Wolves are territorial. They establish boundaries that define their space. Wolves find their way around in the dark, or in severe weather. They know the best hiding places, safe places. It contributes to identity and security. Wolves use the howl as an auditory fence, a verbal warning that minimizes confrontation and decreases chances of injury. Humans might refer to this as being assertive.

Wolves are dependent. They rely on each other for assistance and survival. Ravens and wolves depend on each other (with feeding calls) to locate and consume prey. They are both are wild and Independent. Mutual dependence (or interdependence) is an important skill in all relations. Therefore, wolves mirror the benefits of facing facts, being assertive, and sharing dependence in relationships.

Wolves also mirror a little about enjoying life. Consider these additional traits and skills normally associated with enjoyment.

Wolves are cooperative. They work together toward constructive and instinctually enjoyable service to each other. Wolves share in parenting activities, like feeding and caring for their young. This requires mutual efforts in getting pleasure from giving to others in order to get what you want.

Wolves are playful. They express ideas and feelings through their behaviors. Wolves play freely, and nobody gets hurt. Non-competitive games, like tag come under this category. Humor and teasing can be included if it doesn't victimize others.

Wolves are curious. They follow a secure feeling when they proceed from home base (what is known) and explore new and different areas (the unknown). This includes questioning, asking, and wondering without fear or anxiety. Wolves are very curious, gathering additional information about their environment, while respecting boundaries.

These six examples illustrate how wolves mirror positive skills about surviving and enjoying life. Consider these in contrast to what humans mirror.

Human mirrors

Daily news accounts suggest that modern humans teach exploitation and neglect to each other. For example, significant negative influences often come from parents, teachers, and life experiences. From these you learn to avoid facing the truth about yourself. Consider these defensive skills that often contribute to unhappiness and depression.

Humans use projection. They protect their ego through a process of attributing one's disowned feelings to others. This is a special type of denial and exploitation. It involves refusing responsibility and assigning it to someone or something else. It also includes prejudice, rejections of intimacy through unwarranted suspicion, jealousy, and injustice-collecting. The behavior of someone using this defense may appear different, strange, or abrasive, but fall within the "letter of the law" of what is considered proper.

It results in obsessive over-involvement with the enemy, a special link of intimacy with predators which results in a merging of boundaries. These people are high in negative thinking: self-doubt, pessimism, and passivity.

Humans use fantasy. They create realities in a dream world when goals cannot be satisfied in everyday existence. This is a special type of neglect and self-betrayal. It is associated with avoiding intimacy, ignoring important facts, and, sometimes taking pride in being different. People who use fantasy are often seen as overly dependent, stubborn, or cold. Many had unhappy childhood experiences.

Fantasy can be useful in planning or rehearsing future actions and for momentary pleasure, like in daydreaming. However, idle fantasy is often used to escape the moment, like when people act helpless (by thinking that nothing can be done) or avoid responsible action (during a crisis).

Some people use excessive forms of projection, acting as predators who seek weak or helpless victims to use as scapegoats. Other people victimize themselves by only seeing the bad within. Can you see any mild versions of these traits in yourself? If not, ask for feedback from an honest and caring relative, friend, or counselor. Ask someone to be your mirror imager.

People who practice excessive fantasy often become victims because they fail to face facts and take responsible action. These victims often suffer from depression and cry "wolf!" in search of someone to rescue them. How do you use your imagination? Do you remember to gather facts? Does fantasy bring you closer to what you want or keep you from it?

Symbolic mirrors

Native Americans observed the wolf and other animals to learn practical and symbolic truths. They most likely saw something familiar and admirable in observing the wolf, like <u>themselves</u>.

In some circles today, the wolf has been elevated to a mythical spiritual guide to be revered, in a desire to see the species protected. To other people, these truths have been dismissed as mere fantasy. The greater truth may be clouded by polarized positions. Ask yourself, "Do I acknowledge and revere that wise part of me that provides inner guidance and discernment?"

Early settlers attributed aspects of evil to the wolf such as, maliciousness, thievery, and murderousness. This was their truth. What they saw wasn't the wolf, they too were seeing <u>themselves</u>.

Projecting negative characteristics onto others only perpetuates the problems of prejudice and contributes to victimization. It blocks self-examination and prevents us from finding lessons in our mistakes. A reluctance to look within is often founded on the following belief: "If people really know who I am, they won't like me." Are you willing to look within and face your dark side?

I promise if you really get to know someone, you will find things about them you don't like. That's just the way it is. A better question is this: If you really get to know me will you love me anyway, even if you see some things about me you don't like?

Higher truths reflect unity. They are uniting, not divisive. For example, there is a part in each of us that is wild. It is instinctive and protective. It can be trusted. Also, that part can be savage, insensitive, murderous, and evil, when unleashed excessively and inappropriately. We can monitor and control these traits only when we face them, own up to them, and decide to express them positively. The wild traits can be both trusted and not trusted.

Creating mythical or Disneyland characters can be problematic. This happens when your close relationships are based more on fantasy than reality. You set yourself up for victimization and exploitation. We can benefit most by looking at the wolf, others, and ourselves realistically.

The truth is that we are all animals. Wolves and humans are both wild and civilized. Having consciousness, you can choose to grow and be your best self. Let the wolves live in the wild. This is their nature.

Depression gets your attention. It is a major health problem. However, through seeking therapy, it can offer an opportunity to know your true nature: wild and tame, good and bad, human and animal. Depression creates a personal crisis that calls you to seek help. Through therapy, you are called to look within, at others, and to nature for survival, healing, and happiness.

Depression often results when people feel a loss of control. We resist feeling out of control and build an identity around the perception of control. When chaos surfaces, we respond with a powerful resistance to it and attempt to control it. The human psyche mirrors the physical universe which is basically chaotic and shaped by an underlying mysterious and divine order that some call, "God."

When you begin looking honestly within yourself, you set the stage to find the goodness within. Looking at yourself also helps you identify a true rescuer and guide who saves you from predators and reduces victimization in this world. Lighten up your life by walking through the darkness of your mind. Learn to love the dark into light and learn the positive lessons. As this occurs, you will be able to claim your true nature as a gentle, loving creation.

Who we are at any given moment is defined by the part of our personality that is in control. We move from one part to another, from identity to identity. Collectively, our personality is composed of all these parts.

Future lessons: Who we will become

Erik Erikson, who studied the developmental phases of life, suggested that ego integrity was the highest achievement of the final stage of life. Beginning before the retirement years, this final stage is a time when people begin to reflect back on their lives, review their ups and downs, and integrate their memories and experiences into a final picture of themselves and the world around them. People's integrity reflects all that they have been, done, and achieved. The emerging strength of this stage is wisdom. Failure to achieve a certain integrity of self leaves an aging person facing a gnawing sense of despair.

Reflections of integrity

In my reflections on integrity, I came to believe that integrity was crucial to my mental health.

John Beebe wrote that an excessive concern for the <u>appearance</u> of integrity (image) reflects a dark side of integrity. Another negative reflection of integrity is excessive compromise or caving in with matters of principle. Integrity involves being true to oneself in times of both abundance and limitation. Integrity is a harmony of personal expression with psychological reality: of act with desire, of word with thought, of face with mind, of the outer with the inner self. Integrity is fully realized in terms of continuity.

Therefore, people of integrity are continuous people. For them, the present is a center point on a line drawn out from the left of past memories and to the right toward a willed future. In contrast, people without integrity mirror a chaotic life-style which seems to operate under its own laws. People with integrity have a sense of eternal, universal laws and keep worldly success in perspective. They police themselves. Integrity cannot survive without an attitude of vigilance. People with integrity are always preserving their integrity from the temptations of excessive compromise.

Why must we monitor our compromises? Like most children, I was just thrown into this life, my family and culture without any input (as best I can remember). My childhood experiences demanded compromises of integrity as I learned to survive. In our early experiences, we have all sold out in one way or another. These early survival patterns are difficult to break.

How do we restore integrity? I experienced my parents' guiding me largely through verbal commands, scolding, or spanking. The consequence of this is that my mind, especially the conscience, became filled with those auditory memories and often specific words that were spoken by my parents (and parent substitutes). I sometimes refer to this as the "voice of my father." We also make references to the "voice of conscience." These voices which often contribute to feelings of anxiety or shame can often help direct us back to integrity. Real shame or guilt leads us to new insights, taking corrective actions, and forming new habits. This is called re-learning. False shame only leaves us feeling defective.

Integrity is also restored through the experience of violation. We may not know we have integrity until it has been violated or compromised. It is through these angry or anxious feelings that we become aware that our principles or sense of integrity have been violated. This often happens when we feel betrayed. Emotional hurts are usually accompanied by anger. Underlying our hurt feelings are unmet emotional desires. We can honor angry feelings as a teacher, a mirror of integrity. Anger and hurt surfaces to teach us what we desire and reminds us to stand up for ourselves.

Respecting ourselves and being willing to stand up for ourselves is crucial to maintaining integrity. Real integrity ultimately depends upon the ability within each of us to display a backbone and stand up for the higher principles that we value in ourselves and others. Failure to stand up for ourselves reduces us to being spineless, which is a form of self-betrayal.

Reverse images

In our effort to restore integrity, we must face the shadow, all those disowned and unloved parts of our personality. The shadow threatens to disintegrate the personality by keeping major parts of the personality split and compartmentalized. Facing the shadow allows the personality to proceed to a higher level of moral development. This also allows us to become good neighbors to the people closest to us, because we are good neighbors to all the parts of our personality, including the undesirable parts.

An experience of betrayal, paradoxically, helps restore integrity. When betrayed, you are tempted to either feel superior or entitled to berate those who betrayed you. To assume this position, you have to live only on the positive side of your faith. Living with your positive faith split from the negative side is like living with your faith in a bubble. You romanticize your beliefs and keep them in a fantasy, apart from real life. When betrayed, your bubble bursts. This leads to cynicism and mistrust, an extreme version of the negative side of faith.

This shadow side of faith increases your confidence that, if you stay close to someone long enough, betrayal will be an issue. Either, they will betray you, you will betray them, or you will betray yourself. It happened more than once so far in my life. Betrayal mirrors self-betrayal. Real faith begins when you decide to trust someone and yourself, knowing that betrayal is inevitable. It's about being sure of what you hope for and certain of what you do not see.

Life and personality are never without a shadow side. As you face the positive and negative sides of faith, you must develop a faith that includes trusting that you can survive the pain of betrayal, forgive, and trust again. This involves putting your faith in the One who has overcome these problems, including faith issues.

Shame and guilt must also be embraced for integrity to be restored. Too much shaming does not lead to corrective actions. It contributes to a belief in one's fundamental unworthiness. It sometimes leads to secrecy and antisocial behavior. At times, too much shame results in a defiant shamelessness. Therefore, shame is healed when it is aired in the light of truth and integrity. Hiding shame gives it power, conceals truths, and leads to more guilt and shame.

Emotional pain drives people to seek treatment. Abstaining from a self-defeating behavior is often recommended as a part of a treatment plan. Treatment for drug and alcohol addiction has a long history of promoting abstinence. With the application of 12-Step principles to other human problems, the idea of abstinence has become increasingly popular. It is from the roots and principles of 12-Step programs that we find guidance for understanding a moral process that is free, yet binding in its acceptance of a Higher Power. This is often expressed as, "Let go and let God." Abstaining from self-defeating behaviors takes away the excess that distracts us from our Higher Power and sense of self as a precious child of God.

Reflections of awareness

As you step toward the future, care must be taken to practice daily reflection to avoid self-deception. There are many ways to deceive ourselves. To avoid self-deception, stay in front of a mirror, always in a speculative mode, watching yourself discover developing truths. Remember that subjectivity and fantasy are always in play. Self-awareness must be maintained.

Consider the following steps to maintain self-awareness. The **first** step is to open ourselves up to the mirror image of our emotional lives. This can be done by watching the shadow self, your darker side which is often reflected in dark moods and negative emotions. In this manner, depression and other dark moods can be teachers. They reflect the darkness within you. One aspect of the dark side has been referred to as the absolute shadow, the evil within us and the world. You must embrace the darkness to find the light. In the final analysis, this is the only way forward.

The **second** step involves becoming aware of traits and characteristics you find unacceptable in others. People who seem to irritate, agitate, or otherwise push our emotional buttons are often mirroring an aspect of our shadow. People sometimes reflect a specific trait in you that you are not willing to accept. They are informal mirror imagers. This often results after having worked hard to rid yourself of a certain trait or bad habit. The person we choose to be creates a dark double, the person we choose not to be. To the degree that you disown it or think you have gotten rid of an undesirable trait, you give it power to operate beneath your level of awareness. Informal mirror imagers can serve to increase our awareness when we understand how to use them.

These mirror imagers may unknowingly act as agents of God. I have had conflicts with someone, such as at work, which led to a decision to move on. In moving, I found myself in a better situation. God guides us through people we don't like just like he works through people we admire. He worked through the Pharaoh of Egypt just as He worked through Moses.

The **third** step involves attending to your dream life. This is another avenue for discovering the shadow. Your dreams can help mirror the status of your integrity. You can see yourself reflected in the many people, animals, and other symbols of your dreams. There you will find images that are difficult to face in the light of day. To do this, you must take the time to journal and analyze your dreams. There is no fixed approach to analyze dreams. It works best to go with the flow, using several alternate approaches.

Fourth, take steps to experience yourself through another person. At times, the most powerful lessons are learned by others who witness our suffering. You often encounter the shadow when you least expect it, such as expressing negative emotions or behaving in an uncharacteristic manner. When you are unhappy with your behavior, it's easy to put yourself down. You need to better understand yourself and separate your worth from your behavior. This is often seen when you treat work as a reflection of your self-worth. To avoid excessive pride or pity (depending on your successes or failures), you need honest, direct feedback. You get this most often from a partner or close friend. You also get this in therapy when the counselor mirrors the client's thoughts and feelings to create greater awareness and to reveal blind spots. We all have blind spots. It also happens as a part of working through a twelve-step recovery program with a sponsor. Listen for your lessons from those close to you.

Fifth, build something from the ruins of your ego that often results from self-examination. Recovery involves repairing a shattered, false ego by owning up to negative and positive parts of your personality. From this foundation, you can rebuild an aware ego that controls each personality part with wisdom and humility.

You become your future enlightened self, your best self. These steps can be used as part of a daily plan of action. It involves setting aside time for reflection. This self-examination is necessary in using mirrors as a teacher and maintaining self-awareness.

Other-awareness is also important, especially as it relates to teachers. The wolf's howl is one of many warnings that surface to advise the use of alertness and caution in the presence of dangerous teachings. False teachers will distort the truth for money, pride, or just because it feels good at the moment. There are many who offer simple solutions and quick fixes in exchange for your attention, allegiance, money, and other valuable resources.

How you react to false teachers depends on the situation and the source. At times, disregard or evasive action is enough to protect yourself. At other times, the warning isn't heeded until already drawn in by false teachings. Direct corrective action is necessary, under these conditions. Many people have to detach or distance from the false teachers before effective treatment will work.

To avoid these problems, grow in your knowledge and love for the truth. Reject all teachings that are not grounded in the truth. Discernment is a critical skill in this regard.

Pay attention when a teaching strikes you as strange or unacceptable. This usually means that some additional information has reflected off your prejudices and that a real opportunity for learning may be about to happen. Think twice before you reject new information.

The ultimate lesson: Who we always are

As bits and pieces of information came to me in my growth and development, I began to see life from the viewpoint of the many reflections of the soul instead of just one reflection, the physical dimension. I developed a multidimensional viewpoint. I had previously learned what it is to reflect my energy, my intelligence, and my personality through the physical dimension. I could now reflect these gifts and abilities through many dimensions, including the spiritual.

We live with the limitations of person, time, and space in this life. So much of our time and energy is spent overcoming these physical limitations so we may acquire material things and enjoy more pleasures of the body. Life challenges us to learn how to ground our spiritual self to the physical body and allow the soul to express itself more completely through our bodies. In doing this we experience a sense of timelessness, limitlessness, and preciousness of life by living in the eternal present. We claim our identity as a precious child of God. This results when we learn how to overcome the self-imposed limitations of self-defeating beliefs, emotions, and physical behaviors. In doing this, we become limitless in our ability to love self and others. We reflect the unconditional love of God. We get a sense of the eternal things of life.

I used the observer part of my personality to see life from different viewpoints. Originally, the observer fixed my attention outward to avoid pain and suffering. Next, I learned to use life experiences as a teacher. Later, I looked in the mirror, faced inward past myself, the parts of my personality, and saw my true essence. Through this process, I learned to alter my identity by altering the way I observed it. I became one with life and experienced a healing. I became a healer.

When you see the world as a mirror, you change, and it changes. You may see changes easier in someone close to you. It is not an easy process to measure change. This is why we need mirrors: teachers that reflect lessons and measure learning. As you develop the habit of trusting and taking care of yourself, you will gradually release your old self-defeating patterns from the past. Letting go of the old patterns and habits creates discomfort and, sometimes, can be very painful. This is the pain of re-learning. This pain sets the stage for you to expand your ability to receive and project more love. Soon, you notice that your friends, family, and work associates all are feeling and acting differently. Therefore, you can use the world as a mirror to watch the constantly changing reflections of yourself, as multifaceted, growing and developing toward health and wholeness. You can change the world by changing yourself.

One life experience can significantly alter or shift a viewpoint. When this is a positive shift, we suddenly see ourselves, others, life, and the universe in a positive light. Often, we realize that the only thing that actually changed was the viewpoint. This is why it's critical to learn the positive lessons in negative experiences. Remember, a teacher for a day is like a parent for a lifetime.

Notes

CHAPTER 5

KEYS: HOW TO EMPOWER YOURSELF

Prisons are lonely and frightening places. I worked for eight years at several prisons in Texas providing psychological services to inmates. This experience exposed me to a variety of mental health problems and gave me an in-depth look at people's defensive behavior in a hostile, male-dominated environment. For example, I endured a year of increasing gang activities, chaos, violence, and hostility that was marked by over twenty inmate-on-inmate murders that year. I tried to deny my fears. The following dream illustrates the depth of psychological impact on me:

I am becoming increasingly aware that someone is trying to kill me. Then I am called to evaluate a strange-acting inmate who recently returned from a home visit. The inmate takes me as hostage. I discover he is a leader of a cult gang. I negotiate with him and distract him long enough to escape. Other employees are then taken hostage. I warn the authorities outside, but they will not listen.

I return home. Then cult people begin coming at me from nowhere with knives, one at a time. I successfully defend myself until one little guy just will not quit. We fight until I must cut off his head just to get him to quit stabbing me. I awaken and experience a lingering sensation of stab wounds and knife cuts in my hands and arms, feeling very scared.

The dream reflects what I would not consciously admit, fears and feelings of powerlessness. My well-defended posture at work helped me hide the fears. I had observed some people in that environment routinely using anger, hostility, and brute force to cover their inner fears and feelings of powerlessness. In this sense,

I had close encounters with the dysfunctional behaviors of imprisoned people and their keepers.

I also learned much about the prison sub-culture. It was in prison that I learned that possession of keys is a symbol of status, privilege, and power. Later, in counseling sessions, I also noticed a pattern with clients who misplaced, forgot, or lost their keys. These experiences led me to investigate the symbolism of keys and how people use or forfeit their personal power.

Consider the similarities. Keys are used by wardens to lock doors that hold prisoners. Every day, keys are used to open locks that permit entry through doors. Keys and locks safeguard our valuables so only a chosen few can access them. Although they appear as independent parts, you know that keys, locks, and doors function with unique, inter-related patterns. For example, a car key opens the door and fits the ignition to only one car. The key provides access to tremendous horsepower that moves you across the earth as free and fleet as the wind, with the capacity to carry burdens for great distances with ease. Symbolically, keys represent the cognitive, emotional, and behavioral shifts that click open the doorways to abundant life. Locks represent the self-defeating habits that stifle life. Losing your keys can symbolize losing or giving up your personal power. Empowerment is represented by finding the keys and using them constructively. Dysfunctional relationships can feel like a prison where wardens have taken control and prisoners are expected to submit passively to their authority. The prison runs smoothly while everybody interacts according to expectations.

The following passage from Pat Conroy's book entitled, *The Prince of Tides*, helps articulate this symbolism:

In prisons and mental hospitals, no matter how humanistic or enlightened, keys are the manifest credentials of power, the steel asterisks of freedom and mobility. The march of orderlies and nurses is accompanied by the alienating cacophony of singing keys striking against thighs, annotating the passage of the free. When you find yourself listening to their keys and owning none, you will come close to understanding the white terror of the soul that comes with being banished from all commerce with mankind.

This passage contains symbolism that relates to the quest for keys to unlock doors. There are many doors of loneliness and separation, anger and sadness, or other self-defeating behaviors in life that imprison you in pain and suffering.

In this manner I developed keys as a metaphor for finding, keeping, and using one's freedom of choice and becoming empowered. Through my quest, I came to believe that no one is truly free to choose until they break free from dysfunctional programming of the brain and think for themselves.

In the following sections, several topical areas are addressed that offer insights into how to empower yourself. This leads to claiming more freedom and moving toward a greater appreciation for life, love, and laughter.

Keys to freedom

I learned that contemporary prisons have many unhappy, isolated prisoners who have better relationships with animals than with other people. Even in solitary confinement, prisoners would befriend a mouse, spider, or cockroach and hate their neighbor.

Some "free world" people are imprisoned by careers, families, possessions, or other life circumstances. After a while, even marriage can sometimes feel comparable to a prison sentence instead of a happy journey. For example, two people marry, and the couple's home becomes a prison where the husband acts like a warden and the wife, a prisoner. The warden expects her to show him inordinate amounts of respect, and demands more when she falls short of his expectations. He feels free to make decisions on her behalf, without consulting her. She feels obligated to check with him first. Whether at work or home, these dominance/submission patterns emerge as dysfunctional interactions that feel confining.

Interdependence

There are three crucial dynamics occurring simultaneously in relationships that can contribute to these dysfunctional patterns. The **first** is dependence. Everyone has needs, including the need to be needed. A part of you depends on others like a new born baby depends on his mother. Another part is as dependent on your Higher Power, or God, as an unborn baby is on his mother while in the womb. Problems with dependence occur when the needs are excessive. The **second** dynamic in relationships is independence. There is a uniqueness within you that needs to remain intact and express itself freely. In relationships, respecting one's privacy is the first and most obvious way this need is honored. However, some people are excessively independent and demand an unhealthy amount of privacy. The **third** dynamic is called interdependence. This means people work together to bring out the best in each other by allowing dependence and independence to coexist in the relationship. Love is a key to interdependence. Love calls you to do everything you can to meet a partner's dependent needs without punishing him for having them. Love affirms a partner and empowers him to make personal choices. Love calls you to share power by considering who is affected by your choices, then making mutual decisions or pursuing negotiated agreements. It concentrates on empowerment in relationships with little interest in dominance/submission interactions.

During my employment in the prisons, I was experiencing difficulties in my marriage. Power plays and arguments were frequent, although I did not grow up in a contentious environment. I felt trapped in the marriage because of a sense of responsibility and loyalty modeled by my father. The relationship had become clearly dysfunctional and somewhat abusive. In less than a year after the disturbing dream, I had left both my job and my wife. It took some time for me to realize that I stayed in the marriage so many years for selfish reasons. I sincerely wanted to have a family experience and had been willing to pay the price. However, I had become depressed and lost hope for a better future. Although a difficult decision, I realized the time had come to claim my freedom.

Discernment

If you are trapped in an unhealthy pattern, it is time for you to break free and cease making choices that leave you feeling penitent or confined. This does not necessarily mean that you have to leave anybody. Hidden motives, strong interior impulses, and passionate attractions are so forceful in persuading you to do one thing or another, that without discernment you are not really free to choose. To freely choose, you must have inner freedom. This can only happen when you know what you truly want and allow your feelings to have a say in your decision-making. It also helps to participate when decisions are made that directly impact you.

People who make snap judgments and seek quick solutions often appear decisive. However, it may simply be a habitual response. Hasty decisions can leave you in confining situations. The science of decision-making involves several important steps:

1) Clearly **defining the problem** or issue to be decided;

2) **Developing alternative choices** or solutions;

3) **Evaluating the consequences** of each choice or option; then,

4) **Deciding on a course of action** and implementing it.

Some people take the time later to evaluate the results. Pat Wolff, author of Discernment, adds other important ingredients in the art of choosing well:

5) Taking plenty of **time**;

6) Considering your **head** and your **heart**;

7) Weighing your options against your **values**;

8) Making sure you are free from inner **compulsions**; and finally,

9) Choosing options that are **life-giving** instead of stifling or confining.

Inner compulsions are like old, bad habits. They are often survival mechanisms that have out-lasted their usefulness. These habits become least-action paths through repetition and associating stimulus with automatic response, omitting conscious thought.

Habits

Connecting events and responses can be compared to a spider's web. Like a spider, we consciously choose which events to ignore and which ones to notice based upon experience. By choosing the strongest strands or connecting events with most significance, we make strong associations that are tried and tested until they can be trusted. They become habitual. The spider's survival depends on these strands holding up when the pressure is on. These strands in our minds are the habits, least-action paths that we have created. If they are constructive, they serve us well. When they are self-defeating, they trap us in our own web. We are not free to choose. Decision-making is no simple matter. It can be approached both as an art and a science.

Every emotional wound and stressful experience in life contains the key to enlightenment. You must first learn your lessons and free yourself from personal imprisonment. Only then, you can help others break free. This personal imprisonment includes avoiding your genuine self. When people hide their true selves, they split and go underground. Divided in function, in action, and in their connection with the outer world, they become schizoid. It is no less punishing than a prison. Living without being yourself is like living in a controlled state of schizophrenia. You don't know who you really are. You have brainwashed yourself into believing in a false identity. However, in periods of brilliant insight or when reality shatters your illusions, you realize you have been living a lie. At this point, you know that you must overcome the isolation and break free.

I once attended a weekend personal growth seminar at the request of my friends, who wanted me to check it out. The first session began on a Friday night. The atmosphere had strong overtones of patriarchy: male dominance, tight rules and control, secrecy, and intolerance for questioning. It felt abusive. Soon other participants began asking if what they were doing was what they were "supposed" to do, in a very submissive manner. When I confronted the head trainer about the coercive techniques, another trainer came by me and whispered the word, "control."

On Saturday evening, the atmosphere softened, and everybody started hugging and expressing love. I wondered, "Was this cold-hot approach necessary for my personal growth?" Other questions crossed my mind: "Does this abuse come from the trainer of an older generation?" "Which was the dream, and which was the reality: the abusing or the loving?"

I continued to question the approach in front of the group and was labeled as a trouble maker by the trainers. I was told I was not doing it right. Before it was over, I was ganged up on by four of the trainers and confronted. When the training was over, I couldn't get away fast enough. Every instinct told me this was abusive and dysfunctional, even though the other participants couldn't see it.

Later, confirmation came from many sources, including a magazine article describing the techniques of white collar cults promoted under the guise of personal growth seminars. The lesson from this: No training, therapy, education, religion, job, or relationship is justified in deliberately abusing or inflicting pain in the name of helping, especially without careful and detailed historical information and without licensed, trained helpers.

All people of the world are alike in that they share an equal bond of pain, loneliness, and hunger for love and freedom. Although some people live under different kinds of bondage, there is a spirit within each of them that is eternally free. Spirit cannot be restricted by other people or external conditions. Only you can restrict your spirit. You must claim the freedom to express your divine potential. When this happens, you find the strength to rise above any limiting commitments, conditions, or personal habits.

Self-examination

The key to freedom in the outer world is to know and accept freedom in your inner world. As you grasp this truth for yourself, you also hold this truth for people around the world. You can visualize people everywhere accepting their spiritual freedom and manifesting it. In the eighties, communist people gained new freedom showing the power of a collective spirit. It reminds you that through your Higher Power you are all eternally free!

You must take a long, hard look at yourself to learn more of this inner world. Self-examination involves taking time for contemplation. Some people live as if they were sentenced to prison, just doing time. Serving self-imposed sentences in compulsive behaviors such as workaholism, these people complain of not having time to reflect or make changes. Ultimately, you must learn to alternate contemplation with action and translate insight into behavior. It takes effective behavior in the outer world to satisfy your basic needs while aspiring to social and higher motives simultaneously. This involves living in a cycle of action and reflection that, in turn, leads to more effective action.

Your inner world begins in childhood experiences. A parent's job is to provide a safe place from which the child can explore the world. This helps a child form a healthy attachment in relationships. The parents' emotional availability to the child is a key feature in establishing a safe place. This need for emotional security in another person goes with you into adult life.

If a child fails to receive needed safety and security, he makes negative evaluations of self-worth. In addition, certain unconscious beliefs are formed such as: "It's not safe to be me . . . or . . . be angry . . . or . . . enjoy pleasure, etc." The child becomes trapped in anger, fear, guilt, shame, and a host of other negative emotions. A false self emerges to replace the imprisoned inner child who becomes afraid to come out.

Defensive behaviors, such as pretending to be something you are not, are survival patterns that unconsciously shield the inner child from some real or perceived threat. These patterns can feel like strong impulses or compulsions. A key step in growth and recovery involves recognizing the self-defeating nature of your defense mechanisms and changing them. Gradual change is less disruptive to your life-style. It gives you time to become aware of your defenses and see them losing power. The key to gradual change is substitution, not the destruction of your defenses, but their transformation into more constructive, powerful substitutes.

These false selves, who are developed from pretending to be something you are not, can be destructive in relationships. It gets some people into trouble. It happens to many people. Pretending involves dealing in half-truths or avoiding the truth. When used defensively, it arises out of a failure of spirit that compounds the failure when the falseness is recognized. All types of defensive pretending are potentially destructive. They can be particularly destructive when they dictate behavior. Behavior is the key. People who consistently pretend without directing their behavior toward positive change can be most destructive. To avoid this destructive behavior, strive to be yourself and announce your intentions for positive change.

The inner child holds the keys to surviving and living with happiness because it represents the essence of your good nature. By revisiting past wounds, you learn to release the inner child from prison. This happens by releasing yourself from being a prisoner to anything or anybody, including the feeling or compulsion you have to give your keys to someone else. To maintain power over a child or adult, the wardens of society withhold knowledge, threaten violence or psychological harm, and/or keep money out of their hands. They keep their prisoners in poverty. The worst kind is not financial, intellectual, or emotional. It is spiritual poverty that leaves you feeling most empty. Therefore, gaining empowerment and maintaining freedom involves getting honest, facing the emptiness, informing yourself, and establishing financial, emotional, and spiritual security. The inner child holds the keys to spiritual security. To access the inner child, you must look within and face the emptiness.

Relationships

In the outer world, some people symbolically give away their keys in codependent relationships. Occasionally, during a counseling session, an unhappy person will comment on the idea of meeting their 'soulmate'. The general assumption is that a soulmate is someone who has locks that fit your keys and keys to fit your locks. When a soulmate is found, you know it has happened because you can now be loved for whom you are and not for whom you are pretending to be. The assumption continues in believing that each person helps unveil the best part of the other person. It is as if you have found in one person your paradise on earth and you can feel truly safe to be yourself. This is also based on the idea that you are incomplete and need that missing piece to become whole. To summarize, it seems that a soulmate is difficult to find. There may be only one and it is with this one that you can share your deepest longings and aspirations in life. It is this soulmate that you long for to help make life manifest itself.

These are misconceptions. There is no such thing as a soulmate, in the singular form. You are certain to meet people that you have an instant rapport with and you seem to relate to them in a "special" way. However, when you look for someone to unlock your truest self, you would benefit more to look within, not outside. If you give someone the keys of responsibility for your happiness, then you give them your power of choice. Therefore, who is likely to get the blame when you find yourself unhappy? Your soulmate! This is how some people get disillusioned in relationships. They blame their unhappiness on their mate.

To choose to mate your soul with another soul is your choice. However, you must first become a whole person, and then you can choose who will be your soulmate(s). This need not be limited to one person. The people you choose to mate your soul with can be of the same or opposite sex. You also can choose if the loving relationships become romantic or sexual or if they lead to marriage. If you limit yourself to only one loving relationship, then you leave yourself open to exploitation and closed to a wealth of available love. You define yourself in a limited way by limiting your choices.

Occasionally some people make major life changes when they think they have met their soulmate. Let me continue my stories to illustrate this point. I once attended a wedding that was astrologically planned according to date, time and place. On the way there, I found myself secretly hoping to meet somebody because I was not satisfied in my current relationship. I even had a particular person in mind that I was curious about. Within the hour of arriving, I found this particular woman in my arms and enjoyed it immensely!

The details would only serve to obscure the main point here. However, we openly acknowledged an intense attraction to each other and spent the rest of the evening talking, almost exclusively to each other. I ended the old relationship. Within a week it became apparent that there would be tensions within the new relationship. The attraction was still there, but personal issues and sensitivities seemed to easily get in the way. Two weeks later it was becoming more apparent to me that we were out of sync in our personal journeys through life. We both agreed to end the relationship. Acknowledging this gap between us helped me realize what really happened.

That attraction was like a total eclipse of the sun. The conditions had to be perfect. In a total eclipse, the sun, moon, earth and other heavenly bodies have to be perfectly aligned for the full effect to take place. The people involved also had to be in the same place at the appointed time. It was like clearly seeing the beauty of a bright star in the darkness created by a blocked view of the daytime sun. The star could be seen again, but only either at night or only when the weather conditions were clear or when the moon did not shine too brightly. I realized that to continue trying to re-create those unique conditions under which we met would be futile, frustrating, and crazy-making. We were simply conscious participants in an astrological incident, on more than one level.

It seems that other people have similar experiences in relationships, perhaps without an awareness of the unique alignment or conditions involved that contribute to the attraction. Conditions such as not being fulfilled in the present relationship are often present. They do experience something special in the new relationship and act on it, but fail to let go when it becomes apparent that the experience was a time-limited one. It is as if they fix on a distant star and ignore the daily warmth of a nearby sun. In other words, they endure unwanted and dysfunctional behavior from a person because they can see their potential and imagine how it would be when the other was fixed.

Conditions that contribute to an attraction to a person are often not the ones that we need to sustain a lasting and satisfying relationship. Perhaps from these experiences, we can all learn to better receive what we have in the present moment, enjoy it as a gift and then let it go. This contributes to being able to move on to the next step in our journey and receive the gifts that wait.

It is through relationships that you discover your identity or the nature of your personality. What you call personality can best be defined as a consistent pattern of organization of psychic elements or qualities and traits that are peculiar to each person. Consistency is the key word in this definition. There is a consistency to the personality of individuals that has its dark side and its light side, its good and its bad. The issue of identity, or personality development, usually involves seeing the self as a separate entity. This is particularly important for adolescents as well as codependents. However, codependents tend to define themselves through their relationships, either with people, power, or possessions. This is an illusion. The key to distinguishing between healthy and unhealthy relationships involves this issue of identity development. You must first know who you are and define yourself as a separate entity. This allows you to set healthy boundaries. Eventually, you come to realize that the notion of self as an independent entity is just another illusion. To be free from these illusions, you must realize that you are interdependent with your many selves in the inner world and with your many relationships in the outer world. You must live fully with others to know yourself fully.

To improve relationships, you need to empty yourself of barriers to communication. The process of emptying yourself of these barriers is the key to the transition from "rugged" to "soft" individualism, which is often called interdependence. To learn interdependence, you must first go inward and learn to love, accept and relate to the many parts of your personality, including the unloved parts. The key is relatedness and unconditional love. When these parts are consciously loved and related to, their positive side is manifested. Otherwise their demonic side appears. Avoiding your dark side with denial or rejection of the undesirable parts is exhausting work. Their inevitable intrusiveness and tenacity lead to negative self-evaluations, such as thinking of oneself as bad, evil, or beyond redemption. The key word in facing these many parts is relationship, inner and outer. Both negative and positive parts of the personality are durable traits. This means they do not simply go away or disappear from one's life. They act like permanent partners. To live with the negative aspects, you must find a way to love them unconditionally and keep them under control.

Forgiveness

To love the unloved parts, you must learn to accept your imperfections and forgive. There is a story of a young man who came into a gift boutique, asking to hear the unusual music box in the window of the shop. The owner could not find the key used to wind it. Without the key they could not enjoy the music. It seems that people are like that music box in many ways. You know the gift of forgiveness is available. However, you do not enjoy the peace and joy God has promised because you have not found the key. In other words, you do not think forgiveness is available for you. Perhaps this is because you are often unforgiving toward yourself and other people for the damage you have done or the damage they have done to you and people you love.

In therapy, some clients recall hurtful words their parents said to them as children. Later, they realize that they have been repeating those words to others, repeating the very injustices they were forced to endure as a child. Or, it comes out in marriage counseling that a wife has been harboring resentment and hurt against her husband for years.

These experiences suggest that maybe it's time to heal the memories of unforgiven past hurts. Take the time to reflect on relationships in your life that require healing, including your relationship with yourself. When you realize healing is needed, approach reconciliation in the spirit of forgiveness. In this way you discover the key to unlock the music of God's grace in your life.

Keys to energy

Shamans look for consistent patterns, cycles, and use a vibrational energy, like chants, drums, or music, to transfer illness, take a client's mind off negative thoughts, and bring healing. They are sensitive to the vibrations of their environment. They draw their power from maintaining their well-being, practicing spiritual faith, and by connecting with nature. Consider how dependent humankind is upon our outer world, the environment. Mother Earth provides the basics needed to support life, such as food, air, water, and shelter. All that you need is essentially provided. Yet, some of you have done so little to protect your environment. Perhaps you need a shift in your beliefs and in the understanding of the importance of nature.

Life forces

A key to shifting your awareness and understanding about nature, whether it is human, plant, or animal, is energy. This is a silent reality behind form or physical matter. Within all life is a creative intelligence or Higher Power that many call, God. From the Source, energy flows into the outer world. The essence of the energy that manifests itself in life arises from nature and recycles itself. It is energy that is both life-giving and life-supporting, which is the key to recovering harmony with nature.

Your inner energy is 'ki' (pronounced key), which is a Japanese name for 'life force'." Other cultures have different names for this life force. In Chinese, it is spelled "chi." In Native American Indian culture; it is called "spirit energy." In traditional psychology, it is called "libido." This life force is thought to begin in human life with the piercing of an egg by a sperm cell. From this original fusion, an enormously complex new human being develops. Your life force is a continuous flow of energy linking the various tissues, organs, and brain functions into a unified whole, that begins as an infant being and becomes a human being. This inner life force also links you back to your external environment. Where attention goes, energy flows.

Thought forces

Another source of energy comes from the interaction of thoughts, beliefs, and attitudes with your emotional life. Thoughts lead to emotions, which in turn generate energy. This emotional energy moves you to engage in physical behavior or immobilizes you. For example, fear can fuel your performance to unexpected peaks or freeze you from any response. Therefore, a key to empowerment is maintaining balanced energy in your life. This is about positive mental attitude. You must strive to be conscious of the attitude with which you work on your job, interact in your relationships, invest in your growth and recovery, and carry toward yourself.

Negative attitudes, thoughts, and emotions generate negative energy that powers your self-defeating behaviors. The key to eliminating self-defeating behaviors is to reexamine previously held beliefs and attitudes that no longer serve you well. Attitudes are often difficult to confront because they are unconscious. They must be brought to a level of awareness before they can be consciously examined. At times, professional help is needed to identify and examine irrational attitudes. This careful examination will help you better understand human nature. It may lead to an understanding of the interdependence among you, nature, and Mother Earth that is necessary for survival.

Diverse forces

In relationships, a difference in attitudes and beliefs between people often leads to conflict. The key to minimizing conflict involves learning to transcend individual differences. Learning takes time and teachers. The necessary time for changing behavioral and attitudinal patterns can only be bought through commitment, both to the change and to the relationship. To transcend differences, you also must appreciate and honor diversity. This appreciation of differences leads to the necessary commitment of resources for change: time, money, energy, and conscious effort. Once a commitment is made, teachers can be found in a variety of places, such as positive role models, books, seminars, sponsors, the clergy, and therapists.

In healthy relationships, differences are celebrated as gifts, instead of being ignored, denied, hidden, or judged negatively. These individual differences are often influenced by economic and cultural diversity that also call for positive affirmations and acceptance. Scott Peck, author of The Different Drum, suggests that this acceptance occurs only when you learn how to empty yourself of prejudices and other preconceived notions. This form of emptying is the key to peaceful relationships. When peace and harmony occur in relationships, you set the stage for the power and glory of a unified family of humanity to form. This can appear like the colors of a rainbow following a thunderstorm and offer hope for world peace.

Passionate forces

Initially, loving relationships can be very passionate. Feelings of passion have both sexual and spiritual components. People who respond to passion with sexual expression, without thinking of the consequences, lock themselves into cycles of pain and suffering. It weakens their vitality, drains away their spirit, and, often enrages their partner. It also contributes to the spread of sexually transmitted diseases, which are debilitating the planet. Sooner or later, these prisoners come to realize that, so long as they are ruled by their passions, they are not free within. They have few free choices. Therefore, passion that roars out of control can be very destructive.

Passion that is focused with a sense of commitment can be both spiritual and creative. In the spiritually safe and warm atmosphere of commitment, the power of love builds until it explodes into a new creation. Avoid scattering your energies if you want to manage your passion. In other words, get a focus. Some people need to learn how to acknowledge great passion and love without having to act on it in a habitual and uncommitted pattern. For example, some people develop sexual feelings for a close friend. This does not mean you have to act on them. To learn this lesson sets the stage for managing passion through the boundaries of commitment. It also contributes to healing of fragmented relationships that have been damaged by broken agreements. Therefore, keeping agreements and acting within the bounds of commitment are important skills in managing relationships.

Keys to personal power

An important key to maintaining good health and managing stress is learning to assert yourself. Some people with high stress life-styles have a pattern of doubting themselves or placing a high value on harmonious relationships. These people avoid a direct confrontation and often say "yes" when they want to say "no." They especially need to learn how to say "no" when they don't want to do something, or don't want to tolerate abusive treatment.

Another group of people, without strong personal boundaries, try to please or take care of others. In doing this, they allow others to intrude and take advantage of them. Instead of standing up for themselves and saying "no," they use ill health as a buffer, a way of creating some distance from others. These people try to please others, but seldom please anyone for long.

Ill health is not the only way people avoid using their personal power to get what they want. Some people use things such as sex, food, drugs, or alcohol to indirectly seek what they want. Like nail biting, these are substitutes for love and nurturing. They attempt to feed themselves emotionally with poor substitutes. The key to learning to nurture yourself is to take action on your feelings and intuition. To do this, you must make a conscious effort to tune into how you feel, identify what you want, and risk getting it.

Paradox

Not all indirect approaches, such as seeking substitutes or using ill health, are self-defeating. It is often helpful to use paradox in acting on your feelings. Paradox is a key to healing because it honors the mystery of life. For example, one way to get out of a depression is to go into it. When you feel like doing nothing, the best approach is to do anything. Also, one way to deal with rage is to embrace it. When you own your rage, you can accept it, value it, and work through it to the other side. Just take care what you say and do during a rage. If you have shut down so much emotionally that you quit caring and want for nothing, then simply allow yourself to want something. In this way, indirect or paradoxical actions can lead to feelings of personal power.

Assertiveness

An important key to living with happiness is mastering assertiveness. Assertive people express their thoughts and emotions honestly and in a straightforward manner. This involves feeling-talk, expressing contradictory views, setting healthy limits, and self-starting. Timing is another important aspect of assertiveness. This involves the timely expression of feelings, views, limits, and initiation. Congruence also has to be considered. This involves the match between your words and your non-verbal behavior, such as eye contact, posture, facial expression, and voice inflection.

Dysfunctional application of personal power involves two extremes. The most obvious is aggressiveness. For example, some people come on too strong too quickly and are excessive about threatening or carrying out consequences. These people come across as vindictive, unforgiving, and predatory. In everyday language, we call them, bully. A less obvious misuse of personal power is passiveness. For example, some people fail to express their feelings, especially contradictory thoughts and emotions, and fail to set limits. They intimidate easily and passively accept mistreatment without standing up for themselves. They never get around to consequences. These people are often called, wimp. Each extreme lacks balance and reflects ineffective use of personal power.

How do we recognize when a person has mastered assertiveness? This can only be discerned when viewed from a procedural perspective. Assertiveness is a

~ 139 ~

four-step process. At the **first** step, you request what you want or desire from other people. While waiting for their response, some people might think you are being passive if only observing you at this point. At the **second** step, when your request is still not being honored, you will restate your request and add feeling-talk, such as expressing your anger and hurt. If your request is still not honored, then you take the **third** step. This involves the first two steps and adding a consequence that you both can live with and have control in carrying out. By this time, most people will have honored your request. If not, then you carry out the consequences, which is the **fourth** step. At this point, an observer might think you were being aggressive if that is all they saw. Therefore, when you master assertiveness and learn to use your personal power effectively, people often misinterpret your behavior. However, you and those close to you know you are using it wisely. At each step in the process, remember to affirm your desire to preserve the relationship while you stand up for yourself. This is where mastery becomes evident.

As previously mentioned, there is a spirit that seems to operate in most people that protects and fosters their mental health, like a guardian angel. This angel guards you even under the most adverse circumstances and protects you from harm. However, there can be dark angels that guard, but also imprison your true self, like a prison guard. You imprison and betray yourself. At times, professional help is needed to break the patterns. Through the safety and support of a therapy group or with an individual therapist, you can begin to develop a sense of inner power. This allows you to cease moving through life as a victim who constantly reacts to destructive forces. It offers the option to live as a creative individual who continues growing despite the actions of others around you.

Responsibility

The key is taking responsibility for your actions. When you say, "this happened to me because of what I did," you have power. Accepting responsibility for what someone else did is overly responsible. If what is happening in your life is because of what you are doing, then you have the power to change it. If you think it is because of what someone else is doing, then you are powerless. Therefore, the key to overcoming self-defeating behaviors is not necessarily in having a special knowledge about the recovery process. It is in making an accurate estimate of the percentage of your responsibility. Personal involvement in a community of like-minded people who share their recovery activities is often helpful. However, responsible action, not insight, is the essence and power of the growth and recovery process.

Discipline

Self-discipline is a major part of taking responsible action and developing personal power. This involves conscious effort in abstaining from patterns of dysfunctional and self-defeating behaviors, including gaining control over random impulses. The reduction of pride is the key to progress in recovery and in the development of self-discipline. This can only be done with help from your Higher Power, higher self, and guides. To receive this help, many people benefit from practicing spiritual disciplines. Richard Foster, who writes on the subject, divides the disciplines into the following three categories:

1)   **Inward disciplines:** such as studying, praying, and meditating;

2)   **Outward disciplines:** such as simplicity, submission, and service; and

3)   **Corporate disciplines:** such as confession, guidance, and worshipping.

Practicing spiritual disciplines leads you to recognizing your limited power and humbly asking for help. Paradoxically, admitting your weaknesses leads you to strength when you ask for help. Through the process of overcoming your pride and reducing its active expression, you act with the guidance of your higher self in a responsible, disciplined manner.

Centering

Another way you can regain personal power is through centering. This is a process where a person imagines all parts of the self being brought to the core area of the personality. Here, in the inner world, there is no feeling of being scattered or hassled for the time being. As the result of centering, a person experiences the feeling of safety and empowerment, fully experiencing the present moment, emitting a powerful presence. It is this powerful presence that attracts people to you and propels you into positions of leadership.

Learning

The challenge of wholeness is the journey inward to find your true self and uncover the knowledge within you. If you think your journey is over, resign from your job or get out of your rut. Learning to know yourself is a lifelong process that occurs through all stages of life. Your willingness to be open is what brings you to personal power.

In contemporary times, it is no longer the physically strong person who has power. The person who possesses the most self-knowledge and information is powerful. They are enlightened people. Everyone has the keys to his enlightenment. When you choose to take the journey of enlightenment, you always find guides. Whether you call them, sponsor, spiritual advisor, or therapist, these guides empower you.

The power is always in the person who enters therapy, despite the therapist's competence, mastery of therapeutic techniques, or diagnostic tools. A person decides when to start and end therapy. In turn, a therapist acts as a guide who uses information, sometimes symbolically, that means something unique to that person's life situation. Many people already have the answers to their questions and the solutions to their problems. Therefore, as the therapist listens carefully to the problem, he will learn the answers and the solutions. This instructs therapists to be skillful in empowering their clients. During the process of learning more about himself, a person decides whether to use the information or ignore it. He learns to trust his inner truths and look inside for the answers to his questions and solutions to his problems. He learns to trust his inner authority.

Submission

Tension often arises in relationships regarding the issue of authority or leadership. "Who's going to call the shots?" This becomes the question that often goes unanswered and results in a power struggle. Having both parties in a relationship who are willing to insist on consensual decision-making is a key to the success of the relationship. This translates into sharing your power. Because the life of Christ so clearly calls all people to peacemaking, relying on a Higher Power can be an important key to ending the power struggle and working toward harmony in relationships. This involves two people submitting to a Higher Authority and working toward common agreement. They become co-creators with God.

A key to knowing if you are having a genuinely spiritual interaction in a relationship is that you reach the limits of your willfulness. When limits are reached, and personal willpower alone is not enough, then your self-will can die. At this point, you can relax and allow things to happen. When this occurs, you may experience the energy of love flowing from the interaction. This is why relaxing and getting in touch with your feelings are both so important. The uplifting spirit of unconditional love for God, self, and others is the essence of power. This is the kind of power that conquers fear, anger, and takes the sting out of death. It is through dying that you truly live and love.

How can this be? There are many ways to die. Native Americans believed that when a person looks at a woman as an object or thing to be used, owned, and dominated, he is dead. This also happens when any person looks at another and only sees the bad in them. Or, it happens when a person looks at a forest and sees a potential profit, missing the beauty in the whole thing. In this sense, there are some "walking dead" on our planet these days. When you strive to become your best self, your spiritual heart muscle grows bigger and stronger. However, a heart must relax between beats to function well. In this balance of willfulness/willingness and exertion/relaxation, you become better at understanding, doing and loving. You come alive! You see, hear, and feel the heartbeat of eternal life.

Keys to spiritual power

There is no person more powerful than one who is active and alive in the eternal present, standing up for freedom, goodness, and justice. True spiritual keys come from faith, hope, love, and wisdom. Wisdom involves three parts. It is the art of knowing when to ask for help, how to evaluate the usefulness of the help, and when to accept responsibility for acting on your authority. It is found in remembering your total journey, walking in another's shoes, and being your best self. The results of spiritual power are sharing your gifts, talents, and abilities with love and compassion.

In worldly terms, poverty can keep many people imprisoned and powerless. Spiritual poverty is the most destructive. However, history provides examples of the paradoxical ability of some people to rise from poverty to spiritual power. This happens through sharing one's gifts and talents with love and compassion. Imbued with the power of unconditional love, these spiritual giants are free to fly to the aid of people in need. They overcome poverty with a richness of spirit and carry people's burdens with ease.

Therefore, when you are free from spiritual poverty, you can cease chasing the ownership of people, power, and possessions. This leaves room for unconditional acceptance, which might feel like Heaven. The key to accessing the kingdom of Heaven involves accepting that, without God, you are spiritually impoverished. This is often seen when people become proud of their spiritual accomplishments and forget how God helped them from poverty to plenty. They sometimes look down on those they judge to be spiritually impoverished or undeveloped. Instead of saying, "there but for the grace of God go I," consider using, "there go I and by the grace of God I am better today." This translates into seeing self in others, accepting your imperfections, and freely working toward wholeness by claiming God's grace.

In conclusion, you now have insight into the many keys to empowerment. The doorways are called freedom, energy, personal power, and spiritual power. The keys to freedom are found in both your inner self and outer world. The key to inner freedom is a spirit that arises from re-establishing contact with your essence, the inner child. Contemplation and substituting healthier defensive behaviors help you free the inner child and claim your true identity as a precious child of God, your true essence. The keys to outer freedom involve responsible behaviors achieved through consistency and enlightenment. As these freedoms are claimed, you enjoy better relationships through practicing forgiveness, achieving interdependence, and being emotionally available.

The keys to energy involve connecting with your inner life force and learning to honor all life. This takes a commitment to developing a positive mental attitude that is more accepting of individual differences and group diversity.

In shamanism, the maintenance of one's personal power is fundamental to well-being. This applies to anyone who seeks to be of service to others.

The keys to personal power include mastering assertiveness and taking responsible action. Self-discipline is a primary key that opens the door of personal power. This involves centering and practicing "willingness," including knowing what to do when you reach the limits of your "willfulness." An appreciation for the use of paradox and living with the mystery of life also empowers you. Each of these are keys to becoming your best self.

The key to spiritual power involves the natural simplicity of loving. A primary key is wisdom, which is the ability to use your knowledge with God's love and guidance. True wisdom only comes from God. The last and most powerful keys are faith, hope, and love, with unconditional love being the most powerful. This love only comes from God, but works in its most powerful manner through you or another human being.

I took some risks, left my job and marriage, and moved on to establish a private counseling practice. I love my work. I stayed single for seven years. During this time, I found my way to a loving relationship with myself. Later, I fell in love...with life, nature, and my environment. This led to connecting with a divine love. This loving and satisfying relationship was not without problems, but works best through sharing power and putting love first.

Many people are wounded and hungry for love. Instead of using their woundedness as a doorway through which love may enter, some people seek poor substitutes for love. A key to love is to realize there are no substitutes for love.

Settle for nothing less. Claim the unconditional love that waits for you. Paradoxically, you can then keep it by giving it away. In this manner of living, you freely experience an appreciation for love and laughter. You are free to love life through work, relationships, and play!

Notes

CHAPTER 6

SAFE PLACES: SEEKING EMOTIONAL SECURITY

My interest in the power of place began in the summer of 1987 when I moved to a neighborhood near an undeveloped park. This area provided a solitary place to jog and walk with my black lab, Scarlett. It also provided me an excellent place to stay in touch with nature through the changing seasons. I began to feel rather attached to this spot, yet at the same time wondered why I was drawn to such an ignored place.

Maybe it is because I am introverted and required more peace and quiet than extroverted people. It was this place that I visited when I felt in need of solitude and a natural setting. From the outside it looked similar to the neighboring vacant lots in the area. But when I walked or ran through the trails, I entered a simple yet beautiful garden of wildflowers that provided an array of colors throughout each season. On the ground I noticed petrified wood and pieces of glass turned purple through years of abandonment. The flowers and rocks were graced by several mesquite bushes and towering oak trees. It was here amidst the songs of birds and in the shade of the trees that I came to sit, walk, or jog when the harsh realities of this life oppressed me.

It was a quiet place for a still mind where asphalt and concrete yielded to nature. Serenity flourished as if the cares of the world beyond were just a dream. Here my mind wandered to times past when the wolves and other wildlife were more abundant. Subconsciously, I was reminded of a more peaceful, slower-paced time. A worn path invited me to walk slowly, since this was no place to hurry. It was a place of peacefulness that forbade all haste, a place where the soul spoke and was heard.

My opinions may be biased. I was attached to this place due to a series of seemingly unrelated, but significantly connected events. In October several years prior, I relocated my psychotherapy office closer to my residence, about a block from the park. After Christmas that same year, while visiting Sante Fe, New Mexico, I walked into an art gallery and encountered a most striking painting of a wolf. It was a huge painting of a male wolf that made the hair stand on the back of my neck. In the background were the sounds of Native American flutes playing. I felt a powerful desire for a print since the painting was priced way beyond my budget. So, I left the gallery with my name on the mailing list for a print.

A year passed before I got the print. This was only after I remembered to call the artist with a renewed request. My name must have been misplaced. The print arrived within two weeks and became a Christmas present to myself. It was hung in the office where I worked at the time. It still hangs on the wall of my office. During that same year, I had become interested in wolf sounds and obtained an audio tape from an acquaintance I met at a workshop on Native American spirituality. In addition, a client brought me a poem entitled; Some men are too gentle to live among wolves by James Kavanaugh. By this time, I was openly acknowledging a growing interest in wolves and discussing it with my friends.

During the spring of the next year, while driving past a newly opened bowling alley near the office, I noticed its name, Wolf Pen Creek Bowling. This sent my mind reeling. The car wash nearby was named, Wolf Creek Car Wash. I guessed it! The creek that runs in the park near where I lived, played, and worked for the past several months must be named Wolf Creek. This place was really having a powerful effect on me. Two weeks later I learned that the park was going to be developed and it would be called Wolf Pen Creek Park. I was so excited about these coincidences that I researched the origin of the name of the creek at local libraries. There I discovered that the name probably came from a practice of early settlers who used the creek to pen and destroy wolves.

Additional events occurred that continued to suggest a connection between my consciousness, wolves, and this place. Later, I had a dream involving "honoring the spirit of the wolf." Although the dream was multidimensional, the key focus seemed to be on the idea of "honoring." Another dimension of the dream was realized when I discovered some animal medicine cards in a bookstore that included the exact image of the wolf that was seen in the dream. All this served as confirmation that I was traveling a specific path, but which path?

Other questions ran through my mind. "What am I supposed to learn from this?" I asked. Not knowing exactly what to do, I simply followed my interest in the park, the wolf, and power of place. These connections lead me to taking risks, meeting people, and exploring places that I otherwise would have never experienced. It was through these series of seemingly unrelated coincidences that I came to know my Indian name, Gentle Wolf. Looking back on these experiences, the wolf connection was a way I gave himself permission to attach to this new place I called home. It also gave me an expanded sense of identity. In an unexplainable way, these connections affected my emotional life more deeply by helping me feel more at home with myself and feeling a broader sense of belonging toward the entire planet Earth. The information that follows is a story of what I learned following an interest in the power of place in our lives. I look at this from a psychospiritual perspective and cover several related subjects. I provide answers to the question of how and why we become attached to places and are influenced by the power of place. I hope you will find information that connects to your experiences.

Attachments & place

I had only lived in the area several months when the coincidences began, but I quickly developed a growing attachment to this place. At the time, I had only made two major moves in my life and never actually left an ecosystem referred to the Post Oak Belt that stretches from northeast of Dallas south to the other side of San Antonio, Texas. The first move was after living in one area for 30 years. Each time I moved, I promised myself I would not get attached to the next place, but it happened in spite of my promise.

"Why does this happen?" I asked. Perhaps it's because I lived so long in one place at first. Admittedly, I did want to prevent re-experiencing the pain of leaving a deeply-loved place. In addition, I was accustomed to feeling deeply for my immediate environment.

I later learned that people have always been sensitive to place, but many lost the ability through the years as industry and technology replaced agriculture as a primary livelihood. I also learned that shamans worldwide are sensitive to place and use sacred places, plants, and energies to heal others. Shamans are most powerful in their own countries where they live and work.

An alternate explanation comes from psychological theories of human development, reported by John Bowlby. This researcher concluded that the original function of attachment behavior was protection from predators. First, Bowlby points out that isolated animals are more likely to be attacked by predators than animals which stay together as a group. Second, he draws attention to the fact that, in both humans and other animals, attachment behavior is particularly likely to be elicited when the individual is young, sick, or pregnant. These conditions all make the individual more vulnerable to attack. Third, situations which cause alarm invariably cause people to look around for others with whom to share the danger. In the case of modern humans, physical danger from predators has receded, but the response to psychological and emotional threat remains the same.

So, our attachments come from a need for security and safety. They develop early in life and usually focus on a few specific individuals at first, such as parents and other caregivers. Many attachments endure throughout a large part of the life cycle. We never outgrow the desire to form attachments. This tendency to form attachments with significant persons, places, and things is considered normal behavior for both children and adults. This theory promotes the idea that our principal motivation in life is to connect to something or somebody. It is the chief source of security for many people.

So, the reason I became attached to this place could be due to this human desire to bond with places that provide a sense of safety and security.

Carl Jung, a Swiss psychoanalyst, believed that we all have deep roots that seek to gain geographic harmony. These roots serve to stabilize the psyche, like the roots of a tree. Dr. Jung and others have accented an importance of recognizing the need for obtaining mental harmony with the places where we live and seek true peace.

Typically, people have sought safety and security at home. In many urban and suburban communities, gates and guardhouses have been erected to provide additional security in residential areas. These methods have supplemented existing security methods used in homes, such as guard dogs, neighborhood watch, and electronic alarm systems. Walls and gates give the illusion of security. Critics of the home security movement cite these trends as evidence of a decline in civilization and a return to medieval tribalism. In either case, safety at home is often an illusion when issues of burglary, domestic violence, and child abuse are considered.

In some cases, when things are not going well at home, children seek safety in play, at school, or with pets. However, schools are no longer immune from drugs, street gangs, and violence. Adults tend to seek safety behind their work. Therefore, the workplace has become elevated in importance in modern society. This is reflected in an increased emphasis on the provision of personal services and corporate security in the workplace. However, increased complaints of sexual harassment and discrimination come with this emphasis. So, if not at home, school, or work, then where can security be found?

Third places

It seems some people need a third place. This could be a gathering place that offers a temporary escape from the demands of work and home life. In 18th-century London, prosperous citizens spent many of their free hours in coffeehouses, chatting, exchanging gossip, sipping coffee or chocolate - in short, just hanging out. In our past, American society seems to have had many equivalents of the coffeehouse. Today, Starbucks and other coffee spots serve as places to hang out while students study and stop off places for working people who need a caffeine fix. This accents the need for places where ordinary people can find innocent and cheerful conversation, a very useful diversion to find relief from stress.

The dominant third place in our society has been the tavern. Set it on the golf course and call it a clubhouse. Put it at the water's edge and call it a yacht club. Organize it around creeds and call it a social club. The bar has all too often been the institution that filled this need for a third place. But a third place does not need liquor. It can be established wherever people can gather and linger in peace, such as the park Gentle Wolf discovered.

Consider the importance of physical places in your life. Where do you go when you feel a need for safety and security? Is it home to your parents? Or do you seek out other people? Maybe it is not a person, but a place such as the one described above. Perhaps you look inside, instead of outside yourself. Ask yourself these questions as you investigate the importance of place by using analogies to identify types of safe places and their related substitutes that you create.

Our primary source of emotional security comes from within. It is based upon inner faith and psychological health. Emotional security is also dependent upon past and immediate human relationships, such as family and friends. Geography and other physical attachments are secondary, but are being discussed first. These attachments are usually affected by our level of emotional security. This suggests that a geographic location is less important per se than who we believe is there to reassure us. Therefore, the focus is more on the human need for attachment and how we can express this need in a way that benefits the entire planet.

My first encounter with a specific place led me to take several steps that involved investigating the power other places have had on people. Later, as I discovered more about shamans, I found they soon learn where the power spots are because of their sensitivity to place. I came to own this sensitivity within myself.

Places of power

Carlos Castaneda and other writers have accented the power of certain places. This is often referred to in everyday language as a person being in the right place at the right time, with emphasis being on place more than time. Personal power, preparation of the individual, and willingness to take risks are ingredients that are often overlooked when applying this expression of synchronicity.

In the context of the expression above, power places are spoken of in positive terms. Some places are said to emit earth powers that can be felt as a vibration or tingling sensation in the earth and the air. An energy or energizing feeling is often described that might be similar to the fresh, clean air just after a summer thunderstorm.

I used to feel this way about Austin, Texas, Santa Fe, New Mexico, the Big Bend area of Texas, and Boulder, Colorado. As the cities have become more populated, I feel and see the energy less. When I visited, there seemed to be energy in the air that could be felt and observed in the people. As drug dealers and pollution have increased in the Big Bend area, coming over from Mexico, the energy is less apparent as well.

Certain places have also been identified as negative and harmful places. For example, there are places and environmental conditions around the world that have been identified where the residents suffer greater amounts of depression, fatigue, and suicide. Many are famous, such as the Foehn, a dry southerly wind that blows into Germany and Switzerland out of the Alps in early spring and fall, or the Sirocco which blows off of the Sahara into Italy. In the United States, we are more familiar with the Santa Ana winds in California. These and other places of power have the potential of draining and disturbing people. Therefore, one can develop strange and injurious ties with a locale. These attachments anchor people to a place of power, sometimes for a lifetime, and sometimes to a fault.

Therefore, we must learn to appreciate the effects of place and environment on health and well-being. The earth can be viewed as a life-support system. After all, our best information suggests it is the only place in the universe where life as we know it can thrive. If we alter our perceptions and beliefs about this planet, perhaps we can come to appreciate the environment as sacred and evolve into people who support life more fully.

Sacred places

Native Americans and other native people around the world believe there are sacred places that exist in nature with or without modern people's recognition of their existence. I believe this too. Our society can honor and respect them, ignore them, or say that they simply exist for others' appreciation. If we choose to honor and respect them, and fall into harmony with their power and spirit, the spiritual dimensions of our lives will be enriched. Many people believe that sacred places are foundations of health, well-being, and creativity. When we fail to honor their power, our lives become empty and we disrespect ecological principles. Once the power of the land has become a part of our consciousness, our lives change.

A common quality that sacred places possess is the ability to evoke a special emotional state of mind which modern people call spiritual consciousness. The essence of the spirit that manifests at a sacred place arises from nature itself. Even though many sacred places can be found in the dense cities of Europe, they were often built on the site of earlier temples or nature places that had been previously honored as sacred. People who seem to have the ability to honor sacred places are well-grounded emotionally, have a strong sense of community, divinity, and eternity. They stay attuned to the natural worlds. It is this spirit that is the key to recovering harmony with nature, self, and others. Therefore, it can be beneficial to spend more time with nature.

J.S. Swan says sacred places can be viewed as organs for the Earth to speak with us. Like a mother's breasts, the sacred places nurture us by enabling us to step into states of consciousness in which we realize higher dimensions of reality such as: wisdom, truth, health, and inspiration. Transcendence is normal at sacred places. Unconditional love, whether it is for self or others, cannot exist without transcendence. Sacred places, then, are not just places of power, they are places where we can and do find love from our second mother, the Earth. Many people describe their special experiences at sacred places as feeling the deepest love they have ever known. And love is the correct word to describe what goes on at sacred places when all things are in harmony. This is true because the power of eternal love moves us to become whole, our genuine selves.

In investigating the power of place, I visited a place located on the banks of the Rio Grande River near El Paso, Texas, that was acknowledged as one of these sacred places honored by Native Americans. It is called Indian Hot Springs in honor of several natural springs located there and are considered to have had healing qualities for centuries. Once highly commercialized, this place is now privately owned and seldom used. As I approached the place from the mountains, it seemed there was a modern resort waiting below. This illusion was caused by the white paint on the walls and green roofs on the buildings. On close observation the impressions changed. As I identified the hot springs one by one, it was apparent they had not been used or kept up in quite some time. Some springs were empty. Others were covered with algae. Only one spring near the main house seemed clean enough to sit in. This spring was still warm but there was little room to rest and relax in the water. The hole seemed deep and the water full of minerals. It just seemed sad that it was the only survivor. This place was wounded. It appeared used, abandoned, and wounded.

Is there a lesson in this small example of commercial exploitation and neglect of our natural resources? Other questions arise. What kind of person would allow this? Would a person without emotional security attempt to substitute a physical place for an inner one? Would they have difficulty feeling attached to natural geography and neglect or abuse nature?

Wounded places in our personal lives may not be apparent to other people. But these places of pain are very much with us even though we often try to hide them. However, it may not be apparent to us that these are potentially sacred places. Places of pain can be transformed and become sacred places when we learn the spiritual lesson accompanying the pain and hurts of life.

As a therapist, I have felt both honored and privileged to participate in transforming pain into sacred places. I note a sacred moment when a client shares a fear, concern, or experience that has never been previously shared. It is a moment of trust to be honored. Other sacred moments occur when there is no doubt that a Higher Power is working through helper and the one helped to provide a healing or a major shift in the course of one's life. It is energizing. On a very simple level, a sacred moment is found in the present. I capture those moments with a camera, simply taking pictures to remember that point in time.

Through this process we learn to view pain and other negative emotions from a higher perspective, all being a part of love. It seems that while places can influence us deeply, we have to come to them capable of being touched by them and able to relate to them. Our attempts to seek literal places of significance can be either confounded or helped by our willingness to seek inner emotional security. When we learn these lessons, we can be assured that these wounded places are also sacred places. We become open to relationships.

Places of relationship

It was stated earlier and articulated in detail by John Bowlby that attachments come from a need for security and safety and can endure throughout life. This is normal human behavior that is important in learning to survive in this life with happiness. Therefore, the goal of attachment behavior is to maintain a secure bond or affectional tie with others.

The relationships that are significant to us are usually the specific people we love - spouse or partner, parents, children, close friends, - and sometimes particular places - a home place or personal territory in which we invest similar loving qualities. These significant relationships and the context in which we experience them embody a major part of what we consider meaningful, unique, and difficult to replace about life. To threaten to take them away, or actually lose them results in a loss of meaning and a loss of security. Anxiety increases. These losses sometimes block the ability to find meaning in later life and keep some people stuck in suffering.

Inadequate childhood experiences with parents or other caregivers can lead people either to form anxious attachments or to form very distant attachments. It makes people insecure. This built-in need for attachment gets distorted and results in anxious attachments in which people-pleasing is a primary survival skill.

For example, when mothers threaten their infants and reject physical contact with them, they place children in emotional confusion. Threats such as this stimulate an intense need for attachment in the infant because a prime function of attachment is protection from the threat of danger. But if the source of the threat is the very person to whom the infant must turn for protection, the infant faces a conflict that cannot be resolved. Placed in such a situation, the infant exhibits vacillation between approach, angry protest, despair, and avoidance. This disorganization of behavior is only alleviated by the infant turning away from everything to do with the mother.

Avoidance involves keeping people at an emotional distance. This relates to the fear of being rejected or damaged by hostility and serves to protect the child in threatening circumstances. Anxious submission, on the other hand, is a form of approach behavior. It involves the fear of love being withdrawn. Avoidance suggests doubt in the child's mind if love has ever been given. Anxious submission implies recognition that love is available, but doubts whether it is unconditional. As mentioned, the primary function of attachment is to provide security and safety, to serve as a safe base from which a person can explore the world. Parents must maintain consistent emotional availability in order to serve as a safe base for children. Therefore, when a child has safe ground on which to stand, he can afford to be curious. He can afford to move toward people in intimacy or away in curiosity with ease.

Victims of abuse form an additional kind of attachment. Abusers adopt an attitude of ownership toward their victims. Many victims make the mistake of buying into this line of thinking and develop collusive alliances with the abuser. This happens because a part of the victim believes they lost something valuable to the abuser and will never get it back. Another part believes they were partly responsible for the abuse. For example, victims may consciously or subconsciously believe the abuser took a portion of their childhood innocence. Also lost was a sense of safety and security in a world that they could believe was ultimately managed by a loving, benevolent Deity. The victim feels partly responsible. It seems that this shift in belief gives the abuser more power over their victims. It leads to the victim unknowingly protecting the abuser by keeping the whole thing a secret. This power seems to persist and compete with the concept of a Higher Power, presenting obstacles to finding meaning in life. Beliefs such as this leave a lingering cloud of mistrust and skepticism that overshadows the most caring relationships and retard spiritual growth. These are abusive and harmful beliefs. They must be revisited and challenged before trading them for more constructive alternatives.

Victims form these beliefs during periods of vulnerability, helplessness, and powerlessness in life with many of them being formed before the age of eleven. Other life events such as personal crises and traumatic experiences leave us vulnerable and open to suggestions for a new way of looking at the world. We form positive and negative beliefs about life, places in the world, ourselves, and others, especially those who help us through difficult times. For example, we tend to idolize our parents, children, therapists, or other helpers who aid us during a crisis. We put them on a pedestal. These beliefs get held long past their usefulness. It's important to practice examining our beliefs to see if they still serve us well. Negative beliefs such as the following must be reexamined: "It's not safe to be me;" "Nobody will be there for me;" and "It does no good to talk." Close examination reveals they are self-defeating and either never were true or are no longer true. They are lies.

People only see what they believe. There was a time when the following statement was true: 'A picture is worth a thousand words.' In the age of digital photography and software programs that alter images, this is no longer true. The same is true with therapy. Great truths hold up continuously from the past, to the present and to the future. Great truths live in the now and it is always now. If anyone wants to be healed, they must be willing to surrender their belief systems to greater truths. They must see the lie and upgrade their thinking to a greater present reality. The same is true about the therapists. A client's belief in the therapist enables the therapy to work. A good therapist helps the client grasp greater truths. In addition to therapy, life circumstances bring us new truths, insights, and information that may cause us to become disillusioned about certain places, people, beliefs, ways of life, and so forth. This brings an awakening. It wakes us up. We can no longer hide the truth. It brings discomfort, sadness, and even loss of sleep. This time of sleeplessness has been referred to as the 'hour of the wolf.' Your defenses are down and the wolf can get you. Disillusionment of this kind is not bad; it helps us see a higher level of reality. We face a higher truth. These new dimensions of reality lead us back to the ultimate Reality we call our Higher Power. This is especially significant when we held these very places, people, or beliefs in such high regard that they were worshipped, instead of a Higher Power. Why do we hide from personal and higher truths about ourselves and other relationships?

Hiding places

Abusive experiences yield shame and suffering. The agony of this shame, exposure, and vulnerability triggers our automatic defensive cover-ups. Once these defenses are in place they function automatically and unconsciously, sending our true self, our essence, into hiding. We develop false identities out of this defensive reaction. We become impersonators, hiding behind our survival mechanisms. Therefore, we develop inner hiding places where our true self hides as we live our outer lives projecting our false selves. An extreme example of this would appear when someone develops multiple personalities, which often occurs when a child is exposed to ritualized abuse.

John Bradshaw provides useful insights into these survival mechanisms. Being caught off guard in an abusive, shaming event in childhood creates a lack of self-trust in a child. The child feels emptiness and exposure. He has few boundaries and therefore little protection. He must run and hide to survive. But there is no place to hide since he is totally exposed. They are after him and they are going to take him by surprise and catch him. He's being hunted from moment to moment. These nameless threats are always approaching. There is never a moment when he can relax. He feels he must be constantly guarded. He is alone in the most complete way. As the result of the abuse, the child's self-centeredness will be preserved as a psychological fortress to protect the child against the threats of its intolerable life. We call this type of defense, hypervigilance.

Defenses, while providing safety, also can act as prisons or result in self-defeating behavior patterns in adolescence and adult life. However, we continue to seek places to hide that provide safety and security, either within ourselves or through other people, places, or things.

Occasionally, I saw clients who hid through other relationships and gave to others much of their personal power. In addition, these clients described leaving their body, psychologically, to gain a sense of safety when being abused or feeling threatened. One client described this as 'the hole,' that place where people go when panic strikes.

This hole or gnawing emptiness which we often resist is the point where real change occurs. The hole can be a holy place, if we can come to appreciate both the crazy and sedate qualities of life. However, the false identities perceive the hole as something negative, like death. People often attempt to fill the emptiness with food, drink, sex, work, or relationships. The experience of emptiness or a feeling like something is missing actually shows there is something right, not something wrong. This feeling is the residual contact you have with your essence, your true self.

Other clients have hidden behind the institutions of society, such as the church, military school, college, and social organizations. This urge for safety

~ 163 ~

carries over into jobs, where people will sacrifice their happiness for the financial security of a tenured position in a governmental bureaucracy. It takes something out of you.

The following quote by Helen Epstein illustrates another example of how we build hiding places that both protect and confine:

> I built my iron box carefully, the way we were taught in school that nuclear reactors were built. I conceived lead walls around the dangerous parts, concentric circles of water channels and air ducts that would soften and contain any kind of explosion. I enclosed it all with metal casing and buried the box far away from my brain toward the small of my back, in the part of my body that seemed least alive.

> The box became a vault, collecting in darkness, always collecting, pictures, words, my parents' glances, becoming loaded with weight. It sank deeper as I grew older, so packed with undigested things that finally it became impossible to ignore. I knew the iron box would someday have to be dredged up into the light, opened, its contents sorted out, but I had built such fortifications that it had become inaccessible.

> I needed tricks to get near it, strategies to cut through the belt of numbness that formed each time I made a move toward it. I needed company to look inside it, other voices to confirm that those things I carried inside me were real, that I had not made them up. My parents could not help me with this; they were part of it. Psychiatrists I distrusted; they had even more names to disguise things than I had already tried. There had to be other people like me, who shared what I carried, who had their own version of my iron box. There had to be, I thought, an invisible, silent family scattered about the world.

Modern psychiatric hospitals also provide hiding places for people who seek asylum from the harassments of the world and pressures of daily existence. There remain some shame-based associations with being treated in a psychiatric hospital, but it can be a positive experience. After all, how many places can you go when you need a time-out from life? Priests and other seekers of spiritual growth often take retreats. The word retreat itself may be used to imply a period of time (or time-out) and, by extension, a place which is especially designed for meditation and renewal. Occasionally, a self-imposed period of solitude promotes insights that may be shared with others upon returning to everyday activities. Vacations offer similar places to hide, if we plan them in this manner. Even at work we often find a hiding spot where we cannot be easily reached. Therefore, certain types of hiding places can yield positive results.

Besides psychological and physical hiding places, we also seek to hide in emotional and spiritual places. For example, people often hide their true feelings so well that they lose touch with them completely. People suffering from this problem often come to therapy feeling miserable and unhappy. Their hearts are often closed to both giving and receiving the love they most desperately want. At times, hearts are so closed they are not even able to know they want love. To open up the want, they must learn to open up their hearts.

Places of the heart

Since we tend to hide our true selves, it seems that one way to begin the search is to go into ourselves toward the center of our existence. As we take this step, we become familiar with the complexities of our inner lives. We pay closer attention to ourselves, how we feel, what we think, and what we want. We make ourselves feel at home. When we feel at home in our own house, we discover both the dark corners and the light spots. As this happens, we see the closed doors as well as the drafty rooms and our confusion lessens. Then, we can begin to open the doors of our hearts.

Our false identities, like false beliefs, fix their attention outward toward time, places, images, and people to avoid the trauma of the loss of the real self. They are facing the wrong way or fixed in the wrong time frame. For the false selves to be reabsorbed into the essence or real self, we must look inward and to the present moment.

This inner work involves knowing about ourselves and knowing we know. Henri Nouwen says the key word here is *articulation*. The person who can articulate the movements of this inner life, who can give names to various parts of his personality that drive defensive behaviors, needs no longer to be a victim. At this point, this person is able, slowly and consistently, to remove the obstacles that prevent the spirit of love from entering. He can now create space for a Higher Power whose heart is greater, whose eyes see more, and whose hands can heal more.

Anyone who wants to pay attention has to discover the center of his life in his heart. To do this the heart must open up to giving and receiving love. This involves making peace your only goal. Worry and stress result in a closed heart. An untroubled heart and mind is a safe place to put the insights we gather in life. Among these gatherings are wisdom and caring. It is only through wisdom and skillful caring that we can really pay attention to ourselves. This translates into love.

I learned to use love as healing energy with my clients. It helps form a therapeutic bond. That energy comes from God on the wings of wisdom in a universal manner. All we have to do is suit up, show up, and open the conduit. We channel God's love. The old saying stands the test of time: 'People don't care what you have to say until they know you care.'

We desire to feel as if someone is emotionally there for us. We want contact with another person who will respond to our requests, especially when in distress. The essence of love is a partner who responds to a request, not because it's a good deal, but even when it isn't. This makes us feel as if the world is safe, not dangerous, but a safe place. We feel at home. In matters of the heart, it seems we never grow up.

A greater truth is that we often experience an arrest in our emotional development that keeps us responding to current hurts with immature, childlike responses. When this happens, we are in dire need of an update, a shift in consciousness back to the present. We need a reminder that we are a mature adult and can handle hurts in a much more resourceful manner. We have more options. We are emotionally tougher than a child. We can affirm that we can handle it, get over it, adjust our position, and re-open to love. For some people, the best I can do is love them from a distance. Why do this? It's because life is better when we stay open to love.

In order to keep the heart open to giving and receiving love, people must feel safe. When our safety is threatened, the heart slams shut in a protective response. An alternative is to consider leaving the heart open and moving to a safe distance from the source of threat. This safe distance can be either psychological or physical separation. To work with this, a person must understand the nature of a safe place.

Safe places

We all carry our versions of safety based on life's experiences. We know too much of what is unsafe and wrong with the world sometimes. Knowing too much of what is wrong with the world may cause more pressure than our mind and body can bear. So we develop a safety screen. This safety screen, in our mind, is a place that filters through only as much knowledge as we can safely handle at our present level. What we filter through, we call reality. Each of us has a different reality based on our life experiences. For codependents, these tend to be a black or white reality, which contributes to polarization in relationships. For example, people are viewed as being for or against, helpful or hurtful, and friend or foe. For others, reality may include gray areas, but still remains fragmented and divisive, leaving them feeling lonely and unloved. Many of these people are survivors of childhood neglect or hurt who came to believe that the only way to feel safe is to be totally alone. Therefore, many of our truths about safe places are based on filtered information and survival skills. Neither leads to living with health and happiness in adult life.

As we learn and grow, we can choose to expand the openings of our screen to allow in higher level realities. This results in our own reality changing and we develop a new way of seeing unconditionally. This is the awakening referred to earlier. We come to see safety in connectedness and being willing to ask for help. We learn to stand up for ourselves and care for ourselves better. Therapy can slowly and gently contribute to expansion of new and higher-level dimensions of reality, which include wholeness, connectedness, and unconditional love.

In order to expand these realities, many people seek help through psychotherapy. The therapeutic setting must be safe. This is the therapist's responsibility. I often choose to sit back and listen rather than confront a client. Some people get enough confrontation outside of therapy. Therefore, for the client to open and talk requires a withdrawal of the therapist. One must withdraw to make room for the client. This means the therapist must learn to keep the ego at bay and the heart open.

On the therapeutic level, withdrawal of the therapist aids the client in coming into being. On the human level, by withdrawing into ourselves, out of humility, we create the space for the client to be himself and come to us on his terms. When confrontation is necessary, it can be used as gently as possible in the spirit of love and caring. In this safe atmosphere, clients can feel free to grow and change at their own pace. This seems fair because, after all, they are paying for the service.

To expand reality, we must reclaim our sense of imagination. Paradoxically, as we buy into the idea that there are alternate realities, we slowly give up on the idea that there is a single reality. This takes a conscious attempt to break the social agreement that only one reality exists. It also takes an active imagination.

As people learn to seek safety in higher truths, stand up for themselves, and take better care of themselves, they become more powerful. They are not powerful in a physical or intellectual manner, but powerful spiritually and emotionally. They feel free to express their emotions in an honest and straightforward manner. They are open to giving and receiving love, which is the essence of power. In order to use this power wisely, these people must develop an emotional security that honors the creative intelligence in all life and submit to a Higher Power.

A place of refuge

I admit I often seek divine assistance in working with clients. I discovered that all shamans work with a sense of a higher power. Over time, I learned that many people in a helping role seek Divine assistance. My work became easier as I gradually began to rely on God more and myself less. I'm sure my approach was gentler as I eased up. I ceased to muscle it around so much.

It seems well established that we, in all our trouble and difficulty, need nothing as much as a refuge. This refuge is more than a place to hide, where none and nothing can touch us. The scripture below illustrates the nature of such a place:

He that dwelleth in the secret place of the Most High shall abide under the shadow of the Almighty. - Psalm 41:1.

The scripture teaches us that we can seek refuge in a sure place, known only to our Higher Power and us. It is so private that no power on earth can even find it. We can make this spiritual refuge our home, our dwelling place. Over that home the shadow of our Higher Power can rest, to make it doubly safe, doubly private. Like brooding mother-bird wings the shadow can rest. How safe, how sure we can feel there. When fears assail us, and cares trouble us, then it is because we have ventured out of that protecting shadow of our Higher Power. Then the one and the only thing to do is to creep back into shelter again.

The following quotes from God Calling, by Two Listeners help to add a personal perspective to this place of refuge. These anonymous authors write as if our Higher Power, whom many call God, is speaking directly to us:

Seek safety in My Secret Place. You cannot be touched or harmed there. That is sure. Dwell in My Love. Trust in Me. Know My Divine Power. Laugh and trust. Laughter is a child's faith in God and good.

Cling to thoughts of protection, safety, guidance. Complete surrender of every moment and thought to God is the foundation of happiness; the superstructure is the joy of Communion with Him. And that is, for each, the place, the mansion, I went to prepare for you. All too often you have looked upon that promise as referring only to an After-Life, and too often - far too often - upon this life as a something to be struggled through, in order to get the reward and the joy of the next.

Abide in My Love. An atmosphere of loving understanding to all men. This is your part to carry out, and then I surround you with a protective screen that keeps all evil from you. It is fashioned by your own attitude of mind, words, and deeds, toward others (Two Listeners, 1983).

I love the Psalms and key off the repetition scattered throughout the scriptures of God being my refuge. To me, it's like God is talking to me: 'Learn what it is to shut yourself in the secret place of your being, which is My secret place too. True it is, I wait in many a heart, but so few retire into that inner place of the being to commune with Me. Wherever the soul is, I am. I am actually at the center of every man's being, but, distracted with the things of the sense-life, he finds Me not.' Therefore, my battle cry and my soothing whisper is one in the same: God is my refuge. God Calling is the source for meditations in Alcoholics Anonymous' daily reader called, 24 Hours a Day. Go to these books if you like this approach. Another similar source is Walsh's book called, Conversations with God.

When a situation occurs in life that causes worry or stress, pause for a moment and center your attention on your Higher Power. As you learn to better focus your concentration on the truth of God's presence, you are assured of divine protection.

Many conditions in this world seem less than safe. We pray for the safety and health of our loved ones. As we grow and move through our journey in life, we come to know that we are being guided and protected along the way. Safe passage is provided even in the most difficult times. We study, pray, meditate, and learn to listen. Then we take action and follow through on our Higher Power's instruction with a feeling of protection. Your Higher Power is your protection. But remember, it is what we come to know and believe about our Higher Power, ourselves, our world, that contributes to our ultimate ability to enjoy this protection.

Paths to new places

As stated, a sense of safety and security is a lifelong human desire. Out of this desire, we seek out and attach ourselves to other people, places, or things. When children experience dysfunctional relationships, they often form defense mechanisms that help them survive. These defenses are brought into adulthood because we are attached to them. They are both habitual and protective. Habits can be thought of as least action paths, or paths of least resistance. We have perfected the response so well that we waste little motion or energy. We just react. These paths protect us psychologically, even if they no longer serve us well.

Habits and spiritual disciplines both involve paths of least resistance. They differ from each other by the nature of consciousness and the spirit in which the steps are taken. Habits are often unconscious and acted out in the spirit of fear. Spiritual disciplines are highly conscious and are acted out in the spirit of love.

Out of fear, we learned only too well how to get by with substitutes for loving and caring relationships by submitting to domineering partners or by isolating. We sought places to hide and find ourselves imprisoned psychologically, emotionally, spiritually, and sometimes even physically. We sought refuge and discovered that we have simply run away from our problems again.

Ultimately, we come to examine these paths and places closely to see how well they serve us. The habits that serve us poorly can be exchanged for more constructive ones. This can only happen when we honor the protective nature of all paths and go forward in conscious love. It is from this sense of safety and acceptance that we can take our next step with curiosity and explore the path of personal growth and recovery.

Since beginning my investigation in the power of place and its effect on emotional security, many changes have occurred. Scarlett, the 10-year old black lab who ran with me in Wolf Pen Park, has since departed this life. I continue my path without the pleasure of her company, but I have new companions. I have since moved my residence and offices to other locations. Other close friends have moved on to serve in new places. Each time I lose a friend or companion, by death or other life circumstances, I am often surprised at the loss of security I experience. I anticipate the grief, but the absence of my companions brings an unexpected anxiety or uneasiness. I believe in Bowlby's research. It has face validity. We do seek security in relationships. Knowing this helps me let go when I must, reaffirm present attachments, and move on to form new attachments. This is a work that I embrace these days. I admit that I need dependable, mature people in my life. I work to keep them there and consciously reciprocate.

A major shift in my belief is reflected in the following essay entitled:

To those who didn't notice (my greatest hypocrisy)

To those who never noticed how much I wanted to be a part of your life, your group, or your family, I say, 'thank you.' Thank you for not noticing that I was willing to sacrifice membership in your group and your good opinion of me to take an unpopular stand for what I thought was a higher principle. Thank you for not noticing the pain of loneliness and sting of rejection each time I chose to separate myself from the group instead of blind obedience and acceptance of the dominant point of view. Thanks for not noticing my fear as I stood alone for what I knew, even though no one else could see it.

Thanks, because the loneliness led me to God and God led me to Christ who provided me with the Holy Spirit, who instructed me in the value of right relationships, which led me back to you. It was you who then reminded me that I didn't feel safe with you and this caused me to seek refuge in God. For this I am grateful.

The path to recovery, which begins with an inner focus, can often lead to an outer life that demonstrates a healthy concern for all relations: plants, animals, other people, places, and things. As this occurs, we develop the ability to enjoy and protect physical places as a sort of key to monitoring how well we are doing emotionally and spiritually. In this manner, individual recovery work contributes to the accumulation of a critical mass of recovering people who are leading the entire planet to restoring universal peace, unconditional love, and harmony.

The roots of my insecurities go back to childhood. I had my share of trauma. Much of my childhood was spent feeling sad and lonely. Now, I have formed many attachments and love life. Join us and you need never feel alone again

Fast forward from 1987 to 2017. Thirty years have passed, and this notion of inner safety and security is even more relevant with a national and global backdrop of mass shootings and terroristic attacks. We live in a post-traumatic environment where research suggests about twenty percent develop symptoms.

Notes

CHAPTER 7

BRIDGES: FINDING SAFETY & SUPPORT THROUGH LIFE'S TRANSITIONS

People are lonely because they build walls instead of bridges. This thought reminds me of a former client with an engineering degree who shared a persistent fear of crossing long bridges. The paradox of this prompted a casual, but growing interest in bridges - as a therapeutic analogy that could help guide people through emotional uncertainty to a desired destination. My first step was to follow this concept and notice the use of the analogy in conversation or in reading. Next, I began looking for definitions of the word. I found that a bridge is usually defined as a structure used by people to cross places that are obstacles to travel.

It is a well-known fact that the Romans engineered bridges extensively to expedite the transfer of men and weapons for battle, which gives bridges another connection with fear. So you can see that bridges have different meanings and purposes.

In order to accomplish its common purposes, a bridge must be strong enough to support its own weight as well as the weight of travelers and their possessions. In a children's story, I discovered that instead of an object of fear or a convenience of travel, bridges can also be viewed as structures that provide safe passage between two places. By broadening this latter definition, you might conceptualize the birth canal as representing the first bridge most people cross in life. Therefore, a fear of bridges can paradoxically represent a fear of the very thing which provides desired safety and support. This may also suggest an additional fear of what lies ahead, fear of an uncertain future or the unknown. In either case, I chose to work with a broad definition of bridges in applying it analogously to the idea of seeking safe passages in life's journey.

In reflecting on the symbolism of bridges, I was reminded of the following dream:

I am near a river viewing the clarity of the cold water. I have been camping and am wearing shorts, not a swimsuit. I am standing on a cliff with a friend. I decide to dive into the water. I remove my wallet and we dive in. I am swimming underwater and breathing at the same time. Suddenly, the current is strong. It carries us both down river past a little settlement into a tourist area. Here the river turns into underground caves. There are three caves or channels in this underground area. I can choose any one of the three and end up back upstream, and then go down again.

Somehow, I get separated from my friend who knows the way. I was already worried that someone would find my wallet and keep it. Not knowing the way and being uncomfortable with which channel to take, I ask some people nearby. I didn't trust the one who gave me directions, but acted on them anyway.

I find myself at an opening which required that I go through a section of water in the underground cave. It seems I can no longer breathe under water. I do not know how long I have to swim without air, or if it actually takes me where I want to go, or if I could ever get back. I felt very alone, not knowing, and not sure what to do.

I awaken thinking of the dangers of scuba diving.

I gleaned the following instructions from the dream: stay in charted territory or use guides who know the way; act on the advice of trusted people. It also provided clues to an expanded identity as a shaman, a healer, because of its similarity to a complex, ancient healing technique that involved taking a journey of imagination through an underground stream to retrieve healing powers for clients. I learned shamans often bridge different worlds to assist people in healing. It is called, 'journeying.'

Consider the usefulness of bridges as an analogous way of thinking about safe passages on the path of recovery and personal growth. You cross many bridges as you travel over emotional obstacles and gaps in life. Several will be discussed in the following pages. At some time in your life there has been a teacher, a counselor, a friend, or a wise older person who has provided emotional support and touched your life in a special way. These people may be viewed as bridge builders, or as bridges. Therefore, bridges can appear symbolically in many forms. When we cross them, they usually contribute to emotional convenience or expedite your progress. To apply this analogy to your situation, you must come to believe more in a sense of safety than in fear if you want to safely bridge the gaps, transitions, and cycles of your life.

Bridging life's transitions & other gaps

Ceremonies and rituals have been structured for centuries to provide a safe path for life's transitions. For example, birth is a transition into this world, which carries a variety of rituals. Adolescence is a transition from childhood into adulthood, which often lacks the safety and support of rituals to provide structured passage. Wedding ceremonies bridge two people together. Death and burial rites bridge our mortality with immortality. In short, rituals and ceremonies are symbolic bridges that are structured to provide safe passage from an old and familiar present to a new and uncertain future. Similarly, rituals can provide a safe emotional path to step from old, bad habits to new, better habits.

Change is a part of life, a constant. Everything changes. Security can be found in understanding the changing nature of the universe. Holding on to traditions, old beliefs, or old ways of doing things can result in dogmatism and negative rituals. This happens any time a thought, system, or path has had its time and lost its meaning in the present. Therefore, rituals work best when used with flexibility. Robert Johnson offers the following story as an example of keeping rituals flexible:

Once upon a time there was a ritual for the inner protection and nourishment of the people. The rabbi and all the people of the community went to a particular tree, in a particular forest, in a particular place, on a particular day, and performed a highly prescribed ritual. Then, so the story goes, there were terrible times. A whole generation was scattered, and the ritual was forgotten.

When things got better again, someone remembered that there was an old ritual for protection and nourishment, but he could remember only its overall structure. The rabbi and the people went in to the forest, but they'd forgotten exactly which tree was the right tree. So, they chose a tree and performed the ritual as best they could. And it was sufficient.

More hard times came, and another generation was excluded from the ritual. Somebody remembered that in the old days their ancestors had gone into the forest and done something, so the rabbi and the people went out into the forest and made up a ritual. And it was sufficient.

And then there were more bad times, and much more was lost. The people remembered that in the good old days their ancestors had done something or other, but they didn't know when or what or where. So, they just went out and did the best they could. And it was sufficient.

And there were more hard times, and all that was left was the vague memory that in the olden days somebody had done something. So the new generation went out and improvised and did the best they could, intending their new ritual to be for the protection and nourishment of the people. And it was sufficient.

No matter what you do, whether you do it "right" or "wrong," it will be good enough as long as you do it with flexibility, meaningfulness, consciousness, and in the best way that you know how at the time. This is how to use rituals positively. Begin each one by setting your intentions. In reality, rituals are just something to be doing while you are making conscious contact with God and showing the person being helped that you care and have an organized approach to the process of helping.

Native Americans used rituals in many ways: the sweat lodge as a transition toward purification; a vision quest as a transition toward a greater sense of purpose and connectedness to the universe; and the giveaway ceremony as transition from materialism toward greater spirituality. I learned that a healer goes through a ritual death as part of the initiation. It was an ancient and highly symbolic process that all healers passed through. It marked the death of old ways of life and narrow sense of self and pointed the initiate toward an expanded identity that provided the privilege to heal. Gradually, I realized that many of the changes in my life had been a part of this ancient process. I had crossed many bridges before I became a healer.

To apply this analogy, begin by picturing a bridge in your mind's eye. On one side of the bridge, it is cold and dark, and extremely familiar. You stood there with others in the cold and darkness, experiencing what seemed to be a lifetime of pain and separation. You thought you were trapped on a cliff. Either you did not notice the bridge or were taught to act as if it did not exist, or possibly to believe that only weak people crossed that bridge. However, some of you finally saw the merits of crossing the bridge. You heard of the possibility of healing your pain on the other side. Even though you could barely imagine this, you decided to leave the pain and cross the bridge anyway. As you were crossing, you called back to others on the cliff that there was a bridge to a better place, but they either wouldn't listen or did not believe. So, you decided to go on alone. As you continued across the bridge, you could hear people encouraging you toward the light, warmth, healing, and love. The other side was really a better place. Perhaps you cannot picture yourself in a better place yet. If not, consider the merits of crossing over to the other side.

Bridging generational gaps

If you are a person who has crossed the bridge, there may be a gap between you and those loved ones on the other side. At times, you may desperately try to convince them to cross to this side or you are tempted to go back and drag them over with you. However, no one can be forced across the bridge. Each family member and loved one must go at his or her own choice when the time is right. The choice is theirs, not yours. The best you can do is remind them the bridge is there, love them from a distance, and encourage them as others have done. You do not have to go back to the darkness, pain, and separation because they will not come into the light. You do not have to feel guilt or shame for you have a right to a better life. The best things you can do are stay in the light and reassure others that there is a better place. When others do decide to cross the bridge, you can be there to encourage them to come to the other side. In the meantime, remember you can stay in touch by calling, writing, and sharing your faith, hope, and experiences.

If you still have not crossed the bridge, maybe you can better understand the gap you feel from loved ones who have crossed. You feel the distance because they have changed and may be continuing to grow and change. The path of recovery leads to many bridges. Examples of other bridges are discussed in the following sections. The sooner you cross the first bridge, the more you can believe in the safety of bridges and narrow the gap between you and those loved ones who have gone before you.

Gaps between some loved ones can actually be beneficial. To a certain extent, every family needs generation gaps. These gaps help build healthy boundaries and allow the development of individual identity of young adults. In this case, failures to provide healthy gaps between grandparents, parents, and children can contribute to family enmeshments and retard the maturational process.

It is well known that many problems in families get handed down from one generation to another. It is often helpful to look back into the family history for the origin of current problems.

I had an early curiosity about my ancestors. This was partially because I lost my parents so early in life. Many years were spent researching my family history. I learned more about my ancestors; their origins, their occupations, and their personalities. These activities led me to places and people I would have never seen except for this quest. As a result, I made a greater connection to my ancient grandfathers and lost parents who contributed to my heritage.

A family history or genealogical search can serve as a bridge between relatives cut off by past events. It also can serve as the means for inviting them to cross the bridge. Discussion about dead ancestors can help the family heal old wounds in indirect ways and may serve as a metaphor for the current family situation. Writing letters to collect family history opens up communications with relatives who are often neglected in their later years. In working through unresolved grief issues with deceased ancestors, it can also be helpful to write letters. In either case, these letters can be creative works that address unfinished business with family members. Additionally, they may simply be a way to release angry feelings and say "good-bye."

Hiding problems or failing to communicate about certain subjects in a family constitutes secrecy. Secrecy in families tends to rob ancestors of the right to reach their full potential. It also tends to handicap role identification by denial of information about ancestors. Secrecy obstructs the grieving process when ancestors die. This attitude of secrecy translates into feelings of shame, because "it", the secret, must have been a shameful mistake or unforgivable sin a relative committed. Secrecy prevents honesty, increases suspicion, contributes to mistaken assumptions, and forces a distance among family members. Honest and open sharing through letters and direct conversations serves to overcome the obstacles created by family secrets and opens the way for future communications.

Bridging communication gaps

The primary purposes of communications are to understand and to be understood, to bridge the intellectual and emotional gaps between people. This bridging system can involve either/<u>and</u>/or communication rather than two-dimensional, either/or exchanges. This means you learn to discuss options and look for solutions that help everyone feel like they walk away getting what they desire, not a "my way or the highway" exchange. It also means you learn to see gray areas, not just black and white, when struggling with everyday living problems.

I suggest that if you look with love between black and white, you might even see rainbow colors. The point is to see communications as both transactional and transitional. The focus is on whether or not the listener got the intended message or whether or not the talker even checks to see if the listener got it or even was listening. In other words, it involves looking at the other person's point of view before judging. Therefore, communication is an important part of the healing process. This can be a process that allows you to clarify your wants, present them clearly, and willingly listen to what other people want before coming to a mutual decision. This structure expedites higher level communications.

Communicating can be a fun process that stimulates creativity and imagination. People who use their creative abilities are constantly bridging the gap between the world of external reality and the inner world of mind and emotions. Proponents of the use of creative imagination say that many successful people use their minds to vividly imagine future goals. For example, J.W.

Pennebaker's research suggests there are distinct advantages to the old-fashioned method of communication, writing, to heal past hurts. The act of creative writing can be an avenue to that interior place where, free of pain and doubt, you can confront past traumas and put them to rest to heal both body and mind. Sometimes these hurts from past events can be healed by creatively molding a positive view to the negative event. The use of imagination in creative writing and other expressions of art make people feel that life is worth living and helps to repair losses in symbolic fashion. Therefore, creative writing can be effectively applied to bridge past events with a meaningful present and build positive futures.

I use creative writing for myself and clients. It is one way to uncover pain from small memory fragment of the past. A sample of my work is provided in the steps listed below:

STEP 1: Identify Memory Fragment

"I remember when I was very young that a rooster attacked my little brother. I became angry and cursed. My dad whipped me with a board."

STEP 2: Write a Myth About It

"Once upon a time . . . there were two brothers, ages 3 and 1, who lived in a small rural kingdom inhabited by giants. There were giant cows, giant horses, giant chickens, and a giant rooster who would lie and wait on the pathway for a solitary brother and attack him. For you see, the rooster was larger, meaner, and much more aggressive than a single brother - but the rooster would not attack two brothers at once. Then one day, the older of the two brothers was working on a fence with the father giant. The younger brother was walking along the pathway alone and was attacked by the giant rooster. The older brother was too far away to come to younger brother's aid, but he did express his anger at the rooster -- 'That damned rooster!' Then the father giant picked up a board and whipped the older brother for cursing. Two attacks took place that day....

Many years have passed since this event. The mother giant died a year or two after the attack. Several years later, the father giant also died. And now both brothers are giants, themselves. The older brother became the family hero and spends his time saving family members and others by fighting other giants, but is many times paralyzed by his own anger. The younger brother became the family mascot and continues to entertain people, but feels very lonely at times. He also has a tendency to be like his father giant and punish little sister for simply having and expressing her emotions. One brother now fights giants, the other wounds the inner child . . . ."

STEP 3: Re-write Myth Incorporating Healing Insights

"Once upon a time . . . there were two brothers, ages 3 and 1, who lived in a small rural kingdom inhabited by giants. There were giant cows, giant horses, giant chickens, and a giant rooster who would lie and wait on the pathway for a solitary brother and attack him. For you see, the rooster was larger, meaner, and much more aggressive than a single brother - but the rooster would not attack two brothers at once. Then one day, the older of the two brothers was working on a fence with the father giant. The younger brother was walking along the pathway alone and was attacked by the giant rooster. The older brother seemed too far away to come to younger brother's aid, but he did express his anger at the rooster -- 'That damned rooster!' Then the father giant picked up a board and whipped the older brother for cursing. Two attacks took place that day . . . .

However, there was a spiritual dimension of this event that went almost unnoticed. After the beating, there was a spiritual struggle for the inner child to rise above the occasion and claim a sense of identity as a precious child of God. For what seemed like an instant in eternal measurements ended up being over 30 years before the spiritual response was realized. During this time, the little child was frozen by fear of rejection by the father giant, paralyzed each time he felt angry emotions, and experienced the kingdom as a hostile and threatening place.

Many years have passed since this event. The mother giant died a year or two after the attack. Several years later, the father giant also died. And now both brothers are giants, themselves. The older brother became the family hero and spent a lot of time saving family members and other people by fighting giants, but was many times paralyzed by his own anger. The younger brother became the family clown and continues to entertain people, but feels very lonely at times. He also has a tendency to be like his father giant and punish little sister for simply having and expressing her emotions. One brother now fights giants, the other wounds the inner child . . . ."

The spiritual response has now been released. The older brother previews the old scene and pictures himself looking at little brother, running to him, and rescuing him. The father giant is no longer enraged, but stunned and in awe as he observes the older brother taking a beating, running to rescue the little brother and making a victorious sound that glorifies God!

Healing, such as this, occurs when you share your stories with other people. In the writing, telling and sharing of these stories, relationships are built and healing occurs. Your stories remain silent realities until you share them with other people in a safe and supportive environment. It is in someone else honoring your journey that you find honor instead of shame in your suffering. Then they become real. Creative writing provides the structure to expedite the healing.

A shaman's sense of time is different. Their view overlaps the temporal and mythical worlds, each relating to the globe differently. Myths transcend time. Chronos, the world of experienced time is in the middle of the poles while mythos, the worlds of past and future are at the ends. They are connected as the poles of a magnet, interconnected, but opposite. When you are living your myth, there is a flow, a sense of direction and feeling of certainty about the future. Paradoxically, there is little awareness of present time although you may be very much aware of the eternal present. You do not know where you are going, but you do not care because you know all is well. On the other hand, when you are living fully in the world of experienced time, there is much insecurity, scarcity, and suffering. You care a lot about what is going to happen. This is why myths are so important both to healing and for inspirational living.

Imagination can also be used to cope with current fears and worries. For example, imagine this peaceful scene:

See yourself as a little child in a peaceful meadow of flowers and clover, with protective trees. Visualize a rickety bridge leading over a creek. The other side is dark, unclear, and unknown, but you can cross the bridge, and if you feel frightened you can hold onto supports around you. The bridge rail can be a friend's hand and other supportive people can be beside you on the way.

Life is a series of bridges. You cross new ones as you move from one life phase to another. Sometimes the bridges reach over chasms of pain, of fear, or of sadness. And the only way to make it across is to be supported by something or someone that reminds you that you are not alone.

In your peaceful meadow, you can allow yourself to take a ride on the back of a giant eagle and soar above the bridge to look at the unknown side. It may seem less forbidding than you may fear. When the great bird lands, see yourself dismounting into the hands of loved ones.

Imagination is a mental structure that provides safe passage to overcome fears and face an uncertain future.

We have lost our senses of imagination. They are collectively referred to as our sixth sense, but they are actually five additional senses. The **first** one is the sense of self-healing, like when you cut yourself and your body heals. You can learn to recognize when you are healing yourself. The **second** one is the sense of self-destruction, like when you create problems for yourself through compulsive and addictive behaviors. This is most noticeable during times of low self-esteem, depression, and recent failures. The **third** one is a sense of penetration, like being able to penetrate other realities, other dimensions, other worlds. This is experienced when you notice extraordinary synchronicities in your life as I did when becoming aware of my Indian name. It also happens when you fall in love. The **fourth** one is the sense of perception, like being able to see and understand what you perceive in those other worlds you penetrate. This happens when you can systematically be able to see events and the surrounding world in a different light or assume different points of view. The **last** one is the sense of revelation, like being able to apply what you have perceived when it has been revealed to you. This happens when you can put into words what you understand that has been revealed to you. These five senses of imagination are useful in healing yourself, seeing the future or past, and walking the shaman's path. The sacrifice involves giving up your beliefs that these things are not possible and affirming other possibilities.

Positive, affirming thoughts can be another type of mental bridge. However, these affirmations must be a bridge for two-way, not one-directional, thought traffic. Bridges such as these must be held high, horizontal, and as wide open to receiving as to sending communications. They also must not be elevated on one end so that the rest of the bridge slants down, as if from a superior to an inferior person. This short-circuits the flow of traffic. It is also important to learn to never permit anything but your best thoughts to cross the bridge in the direction of others. When this occurs, thought traffic can be sent back and forth in a natural and mutually helpful way. Therefore, an invisible bridge between two people would indicate that they were in perfect rapport with each other, that they were in a state of real friendship.

Intuition is another type of mental bridge that provides wordless connections. These intuitive bridges can only be formed when you come to realize that regardless of appearances, good is latent in every living thing. This goodness simply needs to be called into active expression through the gracious application of respect, sympathetic understanding, gentleness, and love. Some people believe that intuition or pure thoughts may be seen as angels, whose communications bridge the seen and unseen worlds. Influenced by a small book by J. Allen Boone, I believe that bridges of this type are not built on the type of speech that needs to be uttered, but extend from active functioning intelligent expressions of life that connect from spirit to spirit without demanding any special adjustments. This happens when you strive to be in right relations with others and acknowledge the higher reality of unconditional love. Therefore, communicating effectively creates conditions in which emotions can be released and felt. These emotional gaps must be bridged before you can identify problems within or without and expand your appreciation for all life.

Bridging emotional gaps

Unresolved problems from the past are obstacles to happiness and are often marked by depression. This disabling emotion is associated with feelings of helplessness. It is estimated that ten million Americans suffer from depression and about 30,000 people commit suicide each year. Men over contribute to the suicide statistics.

Because my parents died while I was so young, I suffered a version of mild depression, called dysthymia. It could be simply called, unresolved grief. Many people suffer from other mood disorders of a more serious nature, like major depression, that can lead to death if left untreated. The bridge between depression and suicide is hopelessness. On the positive side, the bridge between depression and happiness is hope, which supports life. Major depression responds best to treatment involving a combination of talking therapy and medication.

Many healers go through periods of suffering. It is part of the initiation and preparation for the work that follows. There are many tests that involve having one's emotional buttons pushed. "A test of fire," I call them. I knew I had passed the test when I could withstand having my emotional buttons pushed really hard and could stand up to mistreatment with love for myself and others without striking back. It was a long process that involved hurt, grief, anger, resentment, and acceptance. Ultimately, goodness prevailed when I learned to live in the spirit of forgiveness.

Paradoxically, depression can lead you to an awareness of the real issues. Awareness begins when people quit holding false hope, start facing the real problem, and make changes. Healing begins when people quit seeking escape in work or relationships and avoid looking for magical cures in things such as drugs or alcohol. Facing your problems means you start talking about your anger and look for the underlying hurts and unmet needs. Next, you share these problems with other people you trust in a safe atmosphere. Only then can you work through the anger and depression and pass on to acceptance and forgiveness.

Forgiveness bridges the gulf of misunderstanding between two people by reinstating access to each other's support. It allows for the release of any negative beliefs, thoughts, and feelings, such as anger, resentment, and grudges. You must face the real source of the hurt or wrong with a genuine release of anger before you are ready to forgive. In order for this to occur, most people must believe two things: 1) angry emotions are not bad or wrong and 2) attacking others out of anger will not get you what you want. It is what you think, say, and do when angry that is destructive. Anger can teach you what you want, if you learn to look at the underlying hurts and unmet desires. Constructive release of anger, admitting your hurts, and working through to forgiveness ultimately leads to emotional renewal and reconciliation. Remember, this also involves self-forgiveness which bridges the gap between the good and bad parts of your personality and helps make you whole. Fragmented and compartmentalized personality parts contribute to being stuck in resentment or denial. If stuck, it often helps to seek assistance from professionals with a healing orientation.

Bridging personality gaps

During my journey, I began a quest to discover what distinguishes shamans from traditional psychotherapists. I found that it is the ability to bridge cultural obstacles and provide healing methods which will treat the whole person. I followed three common threads used in many healing traditions: 1) seeing illness in a holistic sense with a concern for eliciting the client's assistance in the process; 2) the healers acting primarily as a conduit; and 3) acknowledging the influence of a Higher Power in the healing process. Traditional psychotherapists tend to see "pathological" conditions in their clients and work toward "fixing" the problem. As a therapist with a healing orientation, I saw human growth and development as a series of cycles and transitions to be worked through, sometimes with professional assistance and many times without it. In the process of providing an intervention, I was often called to provide a supportive bridge for healing by underlining the client's positive qualities and strengths, while identifying unseen self-defeating traits. Therefore, I worked holistically and saw people as working toward wellness or wholeness, perhaps even holiness. I discovered I was a bridge builder, healer, and a modern shaman. This discovery expanded my identity as a healer. It brought me closer to wholeness.

Why do you seek wholeness? It is because you are fragmented. In fact, you are made up of many selves. Each self is often locked away in a separate compartment, separated by a wall, unable to communicate with other vital parts. This is why the concept that you are made up of different selves is sometimes difficult to understand. Each unhealthy part has a vested interest in keeping a wall up between the other parts. Therefore, some people resist the idea of referring to the human personality in such a fragmented manner.

This is similar to the concept of parallel worlds in quantum physics, except in physics the worlds are physical. From the point of view of the personality, we are all composed of parallel worlds or parts of ourselves. Each one is surrounded by emptiness. Who we are at any given moment is defined by the parallel world we are living in or part of personality that is dominating our consciousness. Under stress, we move toward disintegration. When we are at peace, we move toward integration. Therefore, we live with the illusion or appearance that we have constancy in our state of being when we actually change ourselves according to how we manage stress and have defined who we are and are not at any given moment.

Compartmentalizing the personality helps perpetuate denial and false self-images. However, the general goals in individual and group counseling are to identify the various parts of the personality in order to better integrate your sense of self, bridge what you learn in therapy to daily life experiences, and make healthier life-style choices.

There is an ancient psychospiritual development system called the Enneagram. Although not traditional psychology, it provides the best understandings of the human personality as anything I've found in my career. Embedded in the mysteries of this system is a belief that we move from being to not being, from appearing to disappearing, about 14 times per second. We act as if the disappearance never happens. Compare this process to a movie film which has a space or gap between slides. It moves so rapidly that the gap is not noticed. From the point of view of the personality, the gap is experienced as death, disappearance, the unknown, chaos, or emptiness. The ego resists facing this emptiness and tries to control, hold on, dominate, and fill it up with food, drink, sex, work, or relationships. However, this emptiness can be viewed as a bridge into a much higher level of being by facing the emptiness and getting in touch with your inner child, the essence of your being.

In the process of regaining touch with your inner child, it can be helpful to identify another person besides a psychotherapist to serve as a bridge parent until you develop skills in taking better care of yourself. This person can be any caregiver in society. Many times they are older, wiser, and concerned people who are still watching out for those coming behind them. It is helpful to consider using these parent substitutes as bridges to growth and recovery. In some circles, they are called sponsor, in others, spiritual director, guide, or guru. In either case, they serve to guide, affirm, and nurture you back to health and wholeness. These people are also bridge builders.

In addition to a bridge parent, it is helpful to make conscious contact with your Higher Power. What would you think of a person walking through a beautiful wooded area who fretted because ahead there lay a river and he might be unable to cross it, when all the time, that river was spanned by a bridge? And what if that person had a friend who knew the way, had actually planned the trip and assured him that at no part of the journey would any unforeseen contingency arise, and that all was well?

In daily reading of <u>God Calling</u>, I learned of that friend, your Higher Power, who calls you to leave your foolish fears, follow Him, and determinedly refuse to consider the problems of the past or future. His message to you is, trust and wait.

The following passage from Charles Swindoll's book entitled, <u>Second Wind: A Fresh Run at Life</u> helps accent an additional need for bridges in your life:

For more than forty years I've been running.

The road behind me rambles over rugged and risky terrain. The road beneath offers more of the same. Every road I've taken, every race I've entered has required a strong second wind - that afterburner burst of new hope and fresh determination.

What is it that stirs a second wind? What is it that breathes new energy into your weariness, new vision into your discouragement? For me, it's the feel of a bridge under my stumbling feet. A strong and stable arch to get me through the wastelands and over the washed-out places . . . the low tides, the storms, the winds, the wounds, the aftermath of avalanches.

I'm sure the road ahead won't be much different. I'll still need a second wind. I'll still need a bridge to span the spots I cannot handle alone. The bridge is neither a philosophy nor a dream. The bridge is a person, Christ Jesus, the Lord. The only One who can stabilize me when everyone and everything fades, fails and falls.

Do you know Him . . . I mean really know Him? If so, RUN. Fix your eyes on Him and refuse to give up or turn back. If not, STOP. Give Him your struggles and receive Him by faith. He has all the strength you need to keep you on your road.

Put both feet on the bridge. Meet the real Author of the second wind.

For you who practice the Christian faith, Jesus is the builder of bridges between you and God. He is the Giver of hope that springs eternal. Trust that safe passages have been prepared for you.

The previous references to a Higher Power and bridge builders help further illustrate the need for outside help in bridging the gaps between parts of your personality. Some parts are unknown to you and can only be brought to light with outside help. Many parts drive compulsive and self-defeating behaviors. They block healing. Others are so fragmented that they can only be integrated through a healing intervention. This integration provides passage to integrity, walking like you talk.

Therefore, a bridge builder can be anyone who teaches you something about life or yourself that you might not otherwise have learned. Many times they assist you in re-learning new, better habits. Bridge builders may be a teacher whose work inspires you; a counselor who patiently reaches out to you; or anyone who passes on the legacy of sharing and caring they have experienced from others.

Bridging present with past & future

Bridges appear in many forms. They are often seen in the rituals of life. You have seen historical bridges, mental bridges, and emotional bridges. People can appear both as bridges and bridge builders. Symbolically, they can provide safe passage through times of uncertainty and transition. Practically, they offer support during grief, stress, and changes. While the birth canal may represent the first bridge in this life, death represents the final bridge. Life is about living fully in the eternal present. Failure to do so symbolically results in crossing that final bridge prematurely.

I learned that transitions are a time of movement from what was to what will be. In my life, this involved endings, what is left behind, and beginnings, a time when I could see the changes as gain instead of loss. Using this perspective, I could look back on my life and see that some of my transitions were brief and others took many years. These periods of transition were often marked by increased stress, uncertainty, mistrust, and a limited focus on self-preservation. In order to grow and move forward I learned that I had to reorient myself and engage my new identity as a healer. During these times of uncertainty, I learned to place my trust in myself, others, and my Higher Power to overcome my pain and suffering. I developed a belief that goodness prevails regardless of the circumstances of life. With these tools, I was able to say "good-bye" to aspects of my old self and figure out where I fit in with my new sense of identity as a modern shaman.

Shamans and other healers live in time differently. Just because certain desired realities have not yet manifested in the present does not mean that it isn't coming. It requires a very different way of looking at time and a large dose of faith to pull this off. It's a big stretch if you don't acknowledge the presence of different realities. I understand this faith as the ability to connect with the unseen world, to acknowledge how the unseen has manifested during life, and to remember how clear things can be when looking back on the past. So I remember to honor the past as my teacher, the present as my creation, and the future as my inspiration.

As you move through life and realize the benefit of bridges, perhaps you will become a bridge builder. Acquiring academic degrees, awards, and financial success are a part of the abundance available in this life, but the true measure of success may be found in what you give away or leave behind for those who follow. The quality of their future depends on it.

In conclusion, it seems that sometimes fear of the unknown blocks the passage from a familiar, but undesirable present to better places where greater happiness awaits. Fear focuses on the future. Bridges provide structure and support through uncertain times. Fear blocks people from seeking the support they desire. Insecurity symbolically reduces some people to a position of sleeping under a bridge and emotionally feeding themselves from garbage can relationships. Addictive behaviors can literally reduce people to this state, like the walking dead. There is a land of the living and a land of the dead. The bridge between them is love. Which side of the bridge do you live on? To come to appreciate the safety of bridges and move to your next step of growth and development, you must face your fears, overcome the paralysis, and take action.

As you do this, your heart will open to the unconditional love that patiently waits!

Notes

Some words about the references....

As stated previously, this work has evolved intuitively, initially, in response to a word or concept mentioned in a therapy session and, later, from reading other people's writings. I love to read and have read prolifically through the past 25 years, mostly in the areas of psychology, spirituality, and philosophy. In addition, the training I received in obtaining three college degrees and attending continuing education seminars instilled some of this information in my head.

I use some of the material in this book daily in my work, although it originally came from other authors. I have tried to mention specific authors' work in the text to avoid footnotes or references. These represent the authors whose work I have leaned on heavily or used specific information in their publications. Others are mentioned in the bibliography. Notice that specific scriptures from the Bible are cited for some chapters. Use the "Notes" page at the end of each chapter to take notes or add your thoughts and impressions.

I appreciate the contributions these writers have made to the material you found in this book.

REFERENCES FOR *WOUNDED HEALER*:

Appel, J. (1983). *Cults in America.* New York: Holt, Rinehart & Winston.
Bach, R. (1984). *The Bridge Across Forever.* New York: Dell Publishing Co.
Beattie, M. (1990). *The Language of Letting Go.* New York: Harper-Collins.
Beck, R. (1987). The Genogram as Process. *American Journal of Family Therapy*, 343-451.
Beebe, J. (1992). *Integrity in Depth.* College Station: Texas A&M University Press.
Boone, J. (1954). *Kinship with All Life.* New York: Basic Books.
Bowlby, J. (1982). *Attachment and Loss, 2nd Ed.* New York: Basic Books.
Bradshaw, J. (1980). *Healing the Shame that Binds You.* Flordia: Health Communications, Inc.
Brandenburg, J. (1993). *Brother Wolf: A Forgotten Promise.* Minocqua, WI: Northwood Press.
Burnham, S. (1990). *The Book of Angels.* New York: Ballentine Books.
Carson, D. &. (1988). *Medicine Cards.* Sante Fe, NM: Bear & Company.
Carter, F. (1991). *The Education of Little Tree.* Albuquerque, NM: University of New Mexico Press.
Castendeda, C. (1972). *Journey to Ixtlan: The Lesson.* New York: Washington Square Press.
Chia, M. (1983). *Awaken Healing Energy Through the Tao.* New York: Aurora Press.
Conroy, P. (1986). *The Prince of Tides.* Boston, MA: Houghton Miffllin Publishing.
Epstein, H. (1979). *Children of the Holocaust.* ?: ?
Ferguson, T. (1985). Self-Care. *Post-Graduate Medicine*, 214-216.
Fields, R. W. (1984). *Chop Wood, Carry Water.* Los Angeles, CA: Jeremy P. Tarcher, Inc.
Foster, R. (1978). *Celebration of Discipline: The Path to Spiritual Growth.* New York: Harper & Row.
Foulkes, S. (1964). *Therapeutic Group Analysis.* London: George, Allen & Unwin.
Fuller, E. (1988). *The Courage to Heal.* San Francisco: Harper & Row.
Gawain, S. (1986). *Living in the Light.* San Rafael, CA: New World Library.
Gorski, T. (1989). *Passages Through Recovery.* San Francisco: Harper & Row.
Halgin, R. &. (1989). Understanding and Treating Perfectionistic College Students. *Journal of Counseling & Development*, 222-225.
Hamachek, D. (1990). Evaluating Self-concept and Ego Status in Erikson's Last Three Psychosocial Stages. *Journal of Counseling & Development*, 677-683.
Hammerschlag, C. (1988). *The Dancing Healers.* New York: Harper & Row.
Hemfelt, R. M. (1989). *Love is a Choice.* Nashville, TN: Thomas Nelson, Inc.
Hendricks, G. &. (1985). *Centering & the Art of Intimacy.* New York: Prentice Hall.
Hetherington, C. (1989). *Bringing Your Self to Life.* ?: ?
Holy Bible. (n.d.).
Jung, C. (1963). *Memories, Dreams, and Reflections.* New York: Pantheon Books.
Kavanaugh, J. (1970). *There Are Some Men Too Gentle to Live Among Wolves.* New York: E.P. Dutton.
Kimmel, T. (1993). *Powerful Personalities.* Colorado Springs, CO: Family Publishing.
Larson, E. (1985). *Stage II Recovery.* New York: Harper & Row.
Lightfoot, J. (1934). *Manual of the Lodge.* Fort Worth, TX: Masonic Home & School.
Listeners, T. (1983). *God Calling.* New Jersey: Spire Books.
Marris, P. (1992). *Attachment Across the Life Cycle.* New York: Routedge.

Miller, W. &. (1982). *How to Control Your Drinking.* Alburquegure, NM: University of New Mexico Press.

Muller, W. (1992). *Legacy of the Heart.* New York: Simon & Schuster.

Nelson, G. (1986). *To Dance with God.* New Jersey: Paulist Press.

Nouwen, H. (1979). *The Wounded Healer.* New York: Image Books.

Oldenburg, R. &. (1980). The Essential Hangout. *Psychology Today,* 82-84.

Peck, M. (1983). *People of the Lie.* New York: Simon & Schuster.

Peck, M. (1987). *The Different Drum.* New York: Touchstone.

Pennebaker, J. (1990). *Opening Up: The Healing Power of Confiding in Others.* New York: William Morrow.

Pistole, M. (1989). Attachment: Implications for Counselors. *Journal of Counseling & Development,* 190-193.

Pryor, F. (1989). *The Pryor Report.* ?: Fred Pryor.

Redfield, J. (1993). *The Celestine Prophecy.* New York: Warner Books.

Rower, J. (1987). *The Horned God.* London: Routledge & Kegar Paul, LTD.

Schaef, A. (1981). *Women's Reallity.* San Francisco: Harper & Row.

Shaver, P. &. (1988). A Biased Overview of the Study of Love. *Journal of Personal & Social Relationships,* 473-487.

Silber, K. &. (1982). *Dear Birthmother: Thank You for Our Baby.* San Antonio, TX: Corona Publishing.

Soyka, F. (1977). *The Ion Effect.* New York: Bantam Books.

Starhawk. (1979). *The Spiral Dance.* San Francisco: Harper & Row.

Storr, A. (1988). *Solitude: A Return to the Self.* New York: The Free Press.

Swan, J. (1990). *Sacred Places.* Santa Fe, NM: Bear & Company.

Swindoll, C. (1980). *Second Wind.* Portland, OR: Multnomah Press.

Twohey, D. &. (1995). The Male Voice of Emotional Intimacy. *Journal of Mental Health & Counseling,* 54-62.

Valliant, G. E. (1977). *Adaptation to Life.* Boston: Little, Brown & Company.

Wolf, F. (1991). *The Eagle's Quest.* New York: Simon & Schuster.

Wolff, P. (1993). *Discernment: The Art of Choosing Well.* Liguori, MO: Triumph Books.

Wolinsky, S. (1994). *The Tao of Chaos.* New York: Bramble Books.

Wright, M. (1987). *Behaving as if the God in All Life Mattered.* Jeffersonton, VA: Perelandra.

APPENDIX A

More on Adopting

In the space that follows you will find several additional ideas for self-parenting activities. You are invited to review the list and consider optional activities that you are willing to try in your efforts at learning how to better care for yourself. Remember, you are more likely to maintain sustained effort at activities you enjoy and consider to be fun. Invite your friends, partner, or even your children to assist you in trying on these new behaviors. Taking action and gaining new experiences are necessary steps in breaking old patterns of self-neglect. Have a good time!

IDEAS FOR FREE PARENTING ACTIVITIES

Below are several ideas for free or low-cost parenting activities:

1. Go for a walk
2. Share a hug with a loved one
3. Relax outside
4. Exercise (of your choice)
5. Spiritual prayer
6. Attend a caring support group
7. Practice diaphragmatic breathing
8. Do "stretching" exercises
9. Reflect on your positive qualities, such as "I am..."
10. Watch the sun rise or set
11. Laugh
12. Concentrate on a relaxing scene
13. Enjoy a relaxing nap
14. Reflect with gratitude, such as "I appreciate..."

15. Reflect on, "My most enjoyable memories"

16. Take time to smell the roses (and other flowers

17. Imagine yourself achieving desired goals and dreams

18. Reflect on your successes

19. Write a poem reflecting your feelings

20. Practice a relaxation exercise (or listen to a relaxation tape)

21. Swim/float/wade/relax in a pool/on the beach

22. Create your own unique list of "self-nurturing" activities

23. Enjoy a cool, refreshing glass of water or fruit juice

24. Enjoy the beauty of nature

25. Count your blessings

26. Play as you did as a child

27. Stargaze

28. "Window shop"

29. Daydream

30. Tell yourself the loving words you want to hear from others

31. Practice positive affirmations

32. Pet an animal

33. Smile and say "I LOVE MYSELF...... NO MATTER WHAT"

34. Practice spiritual meditation

35. Practice yoga

36. Sing/hum/whistle a happy tune

37. Swing/slide/teeter totter

38. RELAX: Watch the clouds

39. Visit a park/woods/forest

40. Reflect on "What I value most in life"

41. Go on a picnic in a beautiful setting

42. Practice the art of forgiveness

ADDITIONAL IDEAS FOR PARENTING ACTIVITIES

Below are additional ideas for parenting activities that may have more costs associated with them:

1. Listen to your favorite music
2. Enjoy a long, warm bubble bath
3. Play a musical instrument
4. Do aerobics/dance
5. Visit a place you enjoy
6. Participate in a favorite sport/game/recreation
7. Read positive, motivational literature
8. Go horseback riding
9. Visit a museum/art gallery
10. Treat yourself to a favorite restaurant or cafe
11. Participate in a hobby
12. Reward yourself with a nutritious meal
13. Go sailing/paddleboating
14. Receive a massage
15. Read an enjoyable book
16. Work out with weights/equipment
17. See a special play, movie concert
18. Learn a new skill

ABOUT THE AUTHOR

Billy D. Haddock has worked as a psychotherapist, business consultant, and author. He specialized in the treatment of addictive behaviors, organizational and group dynamics, stress management and suicide. He holds a Ph.D. in educational psychology from Texas A&M University. A licensed professional counselor with over 30 years' experience, he worked in the Texas prisons, at a university, and in private practice. He is now retired and living in College Station, Texas

www.ingramcontent.com/pod-product-compliance
Lightning Source LLC
Chambersburg PA
CBHW060257150626
46556CB00021B/818